# Scattered Hearts

# by:

## The Santa Maria Word Wizards

Coastal Dunes Publishing

Coastal Dunes Publishing
187 Alyssum Circle
Nipomo, CA
93444
http://www.coastaldunespublishing.com

ISBN-13—9780615752938
ISBN-10—0615752934

Published in the United States of America
Publish Date: March 2013

Cover Artist: Barbara M. Hodges

Cover Art Copyright by Coastal Dunes Publishing 2013

# Table of Contents

## Dedicated to Elaine Bierbaurer
June 12, 1922 - October 10, 2003

by: Ann Schafer

All of us who knew Elaine Bierbauer well, know that to her writing was as much a necessary part of life as breathing or eating. When she moved to the Central Coast of California from the southern part of the state, one of the first things she did was to search for a writing group similar to the one to which she had belonged. Finding none available, she and a friend decided to establish such a group in this area. Thus, Elaine Bierbauer might be called the 'Founding Mother' of the Word Wizards of Santa Maria.

Little by little, our group added members, and like all good mothers, Elaine watched over us. Just as all mothers do, she generously praised our accomplishments. When one of us committed an especially grievous faux pas in his or her writing, she would shake her head and say, "You can't do that." And then, kindly but firmly, she would help the wayward writer discover a way to improve the written words.

Mindful of all we owe to her, we dedicate this book—a collection of poetry, short stories, and articles—to her with the anticipation that you, our readers, will find it enjoyable. As you are reading it, we hope none of you will hear a faint whisper on the wind chastising the writer with, "No, no. Didn't I tell you? You can't do that?"

## Who Was Saint Valentine?

by:  Ann Schafer

Claudius II needed strong, young men to fill the ranks of his Roman legions.  There weren't enough volunteers, however, to replace all the soldiers lost in battle; so Claudius issued an edict that all single, young men were to remain unmarried.  He reasoned that unmarried men would be more willing to seek their fortunes on the battlefield than those who would be leaving wives and children behind.

To add to his troubles, Claudius had another pressing problem.  Many Romans were turning from the worship of their ancient gods to the Christian faith and the belief in only one God.  Claudius devoutly believed in the gods of his ancestors and mercilessly hunted down and persecuted those who preached the new faith.

Among the members of the Christian faith was one Valentinus, or Valentine, as he came to be known.  No one knows when or where he was born, other than that it was in the Roman Empire, nor does anyone know when he converted to Christianity.  Valentine became a priest in the Christian church and defied the ruling Claudius had issued forbidding young men to wed.

Valentine performed marriage ceremonies in secret so as to protect the young couples as well as himself.  For all would suffer the wrath of the emperor if they were found out.  Eventually, it happened.  One night, just as a ceremony was drawing to its conclusion, the sound of marching feet could be heard in the street.  Valentine blessed the married pair and pointed to a ragged curtain hanging against the rear wall.

"In back of that drape there is a small opening leading to the alley beyond.  Hurry, and you will be safe."  As the couple ran behind the curtain, the door to the room burst open.  Three burly men entered and surrounded him.

"Where are the ones who were here with you?" the leader shouted. "Where have they gone? We have been told that you're conducting Christian marriage ceremonies in defiance of our mighty emperor, Claudius II. For these disloyal acts, you are to be arrested, and you will be thrown in prison."

Valentine looked at them calmly and replied, "There are no others here. See for yourselves. Where could anyone hide in this small room? If I am to be put in prison for honoring the love between a man and a woman, and for loving and obeying the one true God, then so be it. I am ready to go with you."

One member of the patrol reached over and gave the priest a forceful shove toward the door. "Out with you, Christian dog. We'll see how much love you find in prison."

As the patrol marched him toward the jail, they amused themselves by occasionally thrusting a spear in front of his legs, causing him to fall to his knees. Then, one or the other would reach down and grab Valentine's hair and yank him to his feet. "Here, let me help you up. That didn't hurt, did it?"

"Have you ever seen such a clumsy one?" Another laughed as Valentine struggled to rise after being pushed down for the final time. The jail was just ahead. Valentine was thrust, bruised and bleeding, into a miserable cell and left there to await his fate.

Now, the jailer had a daughter, a pretty girl, but one born with an affliction. Her right foot was twisted to the side, and her right leg was shorter than the left. Her right arm and hand were shrunken and misshapen. Children had always tormented her; even members of her own family shunned her. After all, had not the gods frowned upon her, and upon the entire family, by shaming them with an imperfect child. Having no companions, no friends, Julia spent many of her days with her father. Although he paid her little heed, he, at least, did not tease her. And from time to time, he would allow her to walk through the jail with him, morning and evening, as he spooned food into the prisoners' bowls from the bucket he carried.

This morning, when they reached the cell of the new prisoner, the jailer unlocked the door and handed in a wooden bowl, which he then filled. "Take care of that bowl," he growled. "You will not get another if anything happens to it."

Valentine thanked the jailer, then stood and peered through the open door at Julia. "You are a lovely young woman, just like a ray of sunshine," he said. "Why are you in a place like this? You should be outside where your beauty can be seen by all, although none could admire it more than I."

Julia's eyes filled with tears as she looked at the battered man. These were the first caring words she could remember hearing. "Father, please, may we bring a bowl of water and a cloth to this man so his wounds can be cleansed? He has been kind to me, and I wish to be kind to him in return."

"Perhaps later, when I am free. I dare not let you alone in a cell with a prisoner. Who knows to what horrors he might subject you to."

"Please, father. I know he'll not harm me. Look at the goodness in his face."

"Enough, child. Not until I know more about this man."

When the patrol returned later that day with yet another prisoner for the jailer, he asked them what they knew of the man brought in during the night.

"Oh, he's nothing," one of them replied. "Just one of those Christian dogs the emperor hates. And this one has been marrying couples in defiance of the edict. You should have seen the sport we had in bringing him here. Clumsy ox couldn't stay on his feet." The man laughed aloud at the memory of their journey to the jail.

After securing the newest prisoner in a cell, the jailer decided to examine Valentine more closely. He peered through the opening in the cell door and saw the man on his knees with head bowed.

"I am told you are a Christian. Is that true?"

"Yes, it is." Valentine rose to face the jailer.

"I have heard that Christians are peaceful and do not wish harm to others. Is that true?"

"Yes, that is also true."

"If I permit my daughter to tend your wounds, will she be safe with you? What will you do to her?"

"Only thank her for her goodness of heart and for her kindness to me."

"Well, I will think on it." With this final remark, the jailer turned abruptly and returned to his quarters. Julia was sitting there, staring wistfully through the open door at children playing.

He father looked at her thoughtfully. *She is so lonely. Perhaps it would be good for her to have someone to talk to for a little while. Besides, it would get her out from under my feet as well. And what harm could come to her? No man, not even a Christian, wants anything to do with someone so deformed.*

"Julia, I have decided you may dress the prisoner's wounds, but that is all. Get a basin of water and take some of those cloths." He indicated a pile of dirty rags lying in the corner of the room, clothes that had been stripped from prisoners who had been executed.

Julia hurried to gather the items before her father could change his mind. "I have it all together, father. May we go now?"

The jailer grabbed his ring of keys. "Remember, you are to wash his wounds. Nothing more. And not a word to anyone about this. The emperor would have our heads if he discovered that I let you minister to a prisoner and that one a Christian."

"I promise, father. Besides, people speak to me only to tease me."

When they reached the cell, the jailer unlocked the door, and then entered ahead of Julia.

"My daughter will assist you in washing those cuts on your face and hands. Your cell will remain unlocked so she may leave when the chore is completed, but I will be nearby, so do not think you can escape."

Valentine smiled at the pair standing before him. "I will do nothing to betray your trust. I will do nothing to bring shame upon this lovely young woman who is so kind to me."

Julia placed the basin of cold water on the wooden bench that was the only furnishing in the cell. She laid the rags next to it and searched among them for the cleanest one she could find.  Dipping one end into the basin, she looked at Valentine, sitting near the end of the bench.  "I will wash the dried blood from your face first, since you can't see it.  Then, we will tend to your hands.  How did this happen to you?"

Valentine did not want her to learn of his ordeal, so he replied, "Oh, I stumbled over some object in the street and fell headlong.  I wasn't paying enough attention to what was beneath my feet."

After his face and hands had been attended to, he said, "Now, I will wash my legs and knees.  They also suffered some scrapes.  Next time, I must be more careful."

Soon, the task was completed.  Julia walked to the cell door and called to her father.  She hoped if she did exactly as he asked today, he would let her return the next day and talk to the prisoner.

"Father, I am ready to leave.  All has been cared for as best we could."

The jailer had remained near Valentine's cell but not within sight.  He still did not fully trust the man; and although he felt small regard for his deformed child, still, he did not wish harm to come to her.  "Here I am, girl.  Have you the basin and the cloths?  They must not be found in his cell, and we may need them at another time."

As he closed and locked the door, he said to Valentine, "It's a good thing for you, Christian, that you were true to your word.  Otherwise, harsh and immediate punishment would have been certain."

The next day Julia was allowed to speak to Valentine through the opening in the cell door while her father doled out food to the other prisoners.  Within a few days, Julia was permitted to enter the cell.  Each day, she stayed for a longer period.

As the dreary days passed, Valentine found himself looking forward ever more eagerly to her visits; and he understood more fully the passion felt by the young couples who married despite the danger of being brutally punished by Claudius.

One day, when there seemed nothing left to talk about,

Valentine asked Julia if she knew how to read and write.

"No," she said. "I have no learning at all."

"Well, if your father will let us have writing materials, I can teach you to write your name and some simple words. You might enjoy it."

She was so eager to learn that she ran straight to her father and told him of Valentine's suggestion. The jailer was a man of scant education and was always concerned he might someday get into trouble if he misread an order from Claudius. He reasoned that if Julia gained some knowledge, then it would be to his benefit as well as hers. Therefore, he went to a nearby shop and secured the supplies Valentine had said were necessary for lessons to begin.

As the lessons progressed, the days seemed to fly by. Julia was a bright and willing pupil and learned not only her own name but Valentine's as well. She went on to learn simple words and practiced them over and over until she spelled and read them correctly.

In due course, Valentine received his sentence. Claudius decreed he was to be beaten and then beheaded on the fourteenth of February. Not allowed to say farewell to his beloved, he managed to write her a note and signed it "From your Valentine."

This is the legend of Saint Valentine. How much of it is true, and how much of it is from the imagination of early writers, is impossible to tell. On the other hand, what we do know is that love conquers. Today, no one honors the memory of Claudius II. There is no day set aside, no cards are sent, and nothing is done to remind us of this Roman emperor. But for the insignificant priest, a common man who believed in the power of love, a day is set aside; and his name is celebrated around the world. On the fourteenth of February, how many times will the simple message "From your Valentine" be written?

## Author's Bio: Ann Schafer

Ann Schafer is a free-lance writer and editor who lives on the Central Coast of California. She and her husband moved to this area upon retiring from their careers in southern California. Ann had worked as an administrative secretary for a school district, and her husband had been a high school teacher in the Los Angeles Unified School District. The change in lifestyle gave them time to devote to other pursuits. This was Ann's chance to attempt to fulfill her lifelong dream of being a published writer; and for the past ten years, she has been a regular contributor to the magazine *A New Day*. This has been a wonderful experience—all that she ever hoped for.

## Scattered Hearts and Shattered Dreams

by:  Diane Bechtle

Scattered hearts and shattered dreams.
Loves is often not what it seems.
Longing for passion and sharing
Secretly desperate for someone's caring.
Hopes for closeness and tender touch
Often leaves us wanting much.
Love is filled with quiet expectation
Never noted or given explanation.
And though when it happens it is rare.
It's a gift two souls share.
So accept the noble quest,
Be a warrior with a heart-filled breast.
Love well, matter not the cost.
For in giving nothing is lost.

## Baby Bottles

by: Aubry Johnson

Baby bottles are common and familiar to almost everyone. They come in pastel colors, speak of love and caring. Every time I see babies with their bottles, my memory goes back two score years. To a time before everyone walked around with a cell phone in one hand and a bottle of water in the other. A time when my world was unstable and unpredictable.

*****

Baby bottles full of ice and dripping with condensation, bulged from my flight suit pockets in a very unmilitary manner.

I climbed through 10,000 feet altitude over Da Nang, South Viet Nam. My wingman rode tight and in perfect lock step with my every move. Operation Rolling Thunder was underway. After long and tedious deliberation, the politicians in Washington had decided we would bomb North Viet Nam… again.

The targets all picked in Washington, with more consideration given to politics than to any strategy, frequently were worthless and always dangerous. As proof of this the objective of today's mission lay to the area west of Hanoi, which required an approach through the heaviest concentration of missiles and the biggest group of MIG fighters in the north.

*Do not hit the airfield at Hanoi where all the MIG's are based. Do not fire on anything in the city of Hanoi, where all the missile batteries are located. Let them fire at you, but do not fire back.*

The 'Rules of Engagement' had obviously been promulgated by mad men with the apparent purpose to thin the ranks of Air Force crewmembers. The 'Rules of Engagement' were the orders that permitted fighting a war while remaining socially and politically correct at all times.

13

Correct if you could manage to survive.

On this day, we were armed with AIM-9 Sidewinders for short range, and AIM-7 Sparrow missiles with an effective range of twenty miles. We were required to visually identify any target before firing. And since the Sparrow was not an effective weapon close in, this meant we had to fly up, identify the enemy, than back off twenty miles and shoot.

The moisture caused by the melting ice in my baby bottle was running down my side, melting away even now, just after takeoff.

With the airfield at Da Nang still in sight at my six o'clock position, that vulnerable place behind my tail, I felt the jungle heat insidiously at work.

The baby bottle trick, developed to fight the extreme heat in the cockpit in the steamy Southeast Asia jungles, served to replenish body moisture, at least during the first leg of the flight. The small bottles, usually purchased in the Base Exchange in the Philippines, when filled with water and frozen overnight, made a strange sight bulging from the pockets of the pilots as the walked to their aircraft.

The pastel colored plastic bottles came in blue, pink, and occasionally white, complete with sealing plug and nipple. We discarded the nipples and closed the bottles with the seal caps. The frozen water in the small bottles melted quickly, providing a cool drink to forestall the dehydration that robbed aviators of the wit, wisdom, and alertness necessary to survive the flight into the tiger's mouth.

My bottles had all come in pink, with a heart, lovingly hand drawn on each bottle, a Valentine gift from my wife, Janey. Not exactly the standard cookies from home, but then they hadn't come through the mail, either.

The second of my two scheduled R and R's had come up in February. And because of the increase in direct flights from Honolulu to Da Nang, Hawaii became available to me. I jumped at this chance because Honolulu, of all the available places, allowed me to meet with my wife. So, Janey and I met in Honolulu for five days of rest and relaxation.

*****

The overnight shift from the war to a peaceful American setting was surreal and left me feeling lost and uncertain, with a jagged edge where no edge should be.

This was my time with my wife, but I carried a feeling—or maybe sensation—in direct opposition to what I saw around me.

Air combat is different from what the foot soldier experiences.

The soldier engages the enemy over a prolonged period usually in an unrelenting battle.

Pilots engage and disengage daily.

You get up each morning and pump yourself up for the day's engagement. With each day and each mission, it becomes harder and harder to bring yourself to that fighting edge, until finally you reach the point where, in your gut, you feel the odds have turned against you.

Everyone I know has felt this way about the diminishing odds, but the fact is they never change. They're fifty/fifty each and every day.

Finding myself in the tranquility of Hawaii only one day after a mission where I had watched a man I drank a beer with the night before be blown to pieces, was disconcerting, if not downright overwhelming. This sentience can leave the physiology primed to run, escape, even though the intellect knows everything is right.

While on that R and R with Janey, I found myself looking from the balcony of the hotel at the palm trees swaying gently and the people on the boulevard strolling about unconcerned with bombs or snipers. The difficulty came not from disbelief that it could be so peaceful, but more from the unreality of the whole scene. My first days—marred by my belief that the dream would end and I would wake in that stinking hooch in Da Nang—passed all too quickly.

Janey and I first met in Tokyo where she had been working as a civilian employee of the Air Force. Spending the following five days after we met seeing each other every day made parting the most difficult thing I had ever done.

For the next six months, we wrote regularly but did not see each other until I transferred to California. Coming in one afternoon from a long training flight, I found a letter from Janey in which she asked me to meet her at the Los Angeles airport.

Standing at the gate waiting for Jamey's flight to unload, I was nervous and anxious. Then I spotted her blonde hair bouncing as she walked with her long legged stride toward me and I knew all was well with the world. The first words Janey spoke to me that day were, "Are you going to keep jerking me around, or are you going to marry me and make me an honest woman?"

Of course, I married her. I knew then and there I loved her, and the feeling had never dimmed over the years.

Meeting in Hawaii on this February, Janey and I had to re-establish our relationship made strange by our forced separation. Just as it had happened after other separations, we were tentative with each other. Our lovemaking was bittersweet overlaid with the knowledge that we would soon separate again. Over the years, Janey had endured the moves and the responsibility of making decisions without my help, never complaining. She lived in fear of my flying, but she had known what I did when we married, so she never demurred. Again the love we held for each other carried us through that first frantic albeit hesitant night in Honolulu.

Janey was a dynamo of activity and this explained why her five-foot-five frame never had any excess weight. She had already scheduled our activities for the full five days with a trip to the pineapple fields on the first day. In Wahiawa, on our way the fields, I spotted a watch repair shop and took the opportunity to replace my watch battery.

We walked into the small shop and found it full of clocks, clocks of all sizes and shapes, many setting on crude shelves covered in dust. The quiet of the shop shrouded with a layer of ageless dust exactly matched my confused mood. The dust covered everything. All thought and sound muffled by the omnipresent dust.

Suddenly, surprisingly, one clock chimed, a beautiful upbeat chime that shed dust and antiquity, followed by another and another. Soon the shop was alive with the varied tones of a thousand clocks, each sending out its sounds with great gusto as if to penetrate the layers of dust and cry out, "I'm here, I'm here."

At that moment, Janey slipped her hand into mine. I looked down and saw her smile and I knew I was okay. We were okay.

Just as suddenly, as it started the first clock finished its cycle and another fell silent, until the joyful clamor concluded and the shop was quiet again. Quiet yes, but no longer foreboding, quiet and peaceful with its beauty at rest

After doing the around-the-island tour and other mandatory tourist things, we settled down to a more sedate pace, taking in the sun and recapturing that easy comfort we had always had with each other. Janey and I were best friends; she knew the 'me' no one else ever saw. To my great good fortune, she still loved me. One lazy afternoon, sitting on the lanai of the Royal Hawaiian Hotel, a Mai Tai in my hand I told Janey about the baby bottles.

"I need to find a market before I go back," I said.

"Why do you need a market? Are you going to start cooking in your hooch?"

"No, I need to pick up a few baby bottles."

"Baby bottles? Are you pregnant, or are these for your Vietnamese Butterfly girl?"

"No, no, nothing like that," I protested forcibly. "We put water in the bottles to carry on our flights so we can have drinking water. The little short bottles are just right to fit in the flight suit pockets. All the guys carry them."

Looking at her watch, Janey interrupted my story. "We have to go, or the catamaran will leave without us." The catamaran ride into Pearl Harbor, with a stop at the U.S.S. Arizona memorial, was another mandatory tourist thing. Standing on the over bridge mounted on the sunken ship, watching the oil bubbles rise to the surface, I finished my story of the baby bottles and how they played a part in my life.

Janey listened without comment, and as we became engrossed with the beauty of Hawaii, our conversation moved on to other things.

The bottles dropped out of my mind in the easy days following.

In the terminal at Hickam Air Force Base, located on the military side of Honolulu International, while I waited to climb aboard the C-141 for the flight back to Nam, Janey presented me with a package, complete with red and pink wrapping.

"Open this after you're airborne. It's my gift to you with the hope and prayer that you fly safe always."

It always rocked me when she said this. She had never missed a day when I was leaving on a flight to say, "Fly safe always." She looked at me with her eyes full of love and I could see deep down the fear she strove to conceal. A fear I was aware of but unable to allay. Flying fighters was what I did. She had always known and accepted it as part of me. Janey did not want me to quit for she knew it would change me in ways she would not like, but still, she feared.

In the air somewhere over the Pacific, I opened the package, not knowing what I would find. Janey had always been a very gifted and creative person and had frequently surprised me with her gifts. This one totally blew me away.

There in the box lay six small pink baby bottles each one bearing a small heart meticulously drawn in a contrasting deeper pink color.

Once on the ground at Da Nang, I filled my bottles and placed them in the mess hall kitchen freezer to await my next flight, all the while recalling the tenderness with which Janey had handed me the package.

Just before today's flight, I had met with the supply Sergeant to request another Kevlar flack jacket. Although I had a jacket issued when I arrived in Da Nang, I needed another.

"Sir, you have a jacket on. Why do you need another one?"

"I need one to sit on, Sarg. I need to protect my butt and other important things." The extra jacket would go on the seat to protect me from any random fire from below.

"Well, I don't know Sir. I have to account for this stuff."

"Sure you do, and I have here a bottle of scotch to help with the accounting."

With the necessary military protocol completed, I walked to the flight line with my new baby bottles neatly tucked into my flack vest and in the upper pockets of my flight suit. With all the straps and bindings involved in keeping my body in the ejection seat, access to my pockets became very difficult. Because of the pressure suit worn below the waist to counteract the G force pressures the lower pockets in the flight suit were not usable. In my suit, I had removed the zippers and other protrusions to reduce the discomfort caused when the G-suit inflated.

The cool moisture running down my side as the frozen bottles thawed had a strange, calming effect that helped me endure one more day in hell. The bottles and the coolness I felt were a lifeline to Janey and to sanity. Shifting slightly in the Martin-Baker ejection seat searching for a comfortable position that didn't exist, I heard my wingman call over the radio.

"Tiger lead, you're making smoke."

"Roger," I responded.

The F-4C Phantom II liked to leave a smoke trail, telling the enemy gunners on the ground exactly where it was if they didn't already have it on radar. Knowing how hopeless it was, I made a slight change on the power setting, trying to lose the telltale smoke trail streaming out behind my six, marking my flight path through the sky. Sometimes, not often, a small change in the tail pipe temperature could reduce the smoke trail.

Opening my second bottle, I had barely a sip when my weapons officer in the back seat called on the intercom, "I've got a lock. They've fired one—no—two missiles are in the air!"

Pulling up and going over the top, I separated from my wingman as he split in the opposite direction, and watched the first SAM pass under my wing. Pushing hard on the left rudder pedal, trying to force the beast into a modified hammerhead, I watched the G-meter climb toward the red line, making a thrust reduction necessary. Retarding the power levers to control the forces of gravity made the weight ease off my body and allowed me to search for the second missile.

McDonnell Aircraft had not built a pretty airplane when they put the F-4C Phantom II together, but they had built a solid, tough airplane. The aircraft could take a lot of abuse before it made any protest. The G-meter locked and registered the highest G force during each flight. I had landed more than once with the G-meter maxed against the peg.

"Break left," my backseater called. "She's going to go behind us."

The second missile, climbing above our position, wobbled briefly and self-destructed, lighting up the morning sky. Because of their inherent lack of accuracy, the North Viet Nam gunners had learned to fire in sets of two.

Reforming over Dai Dien, our flight continued north into Uncle Ho's stronghold. I looked with regret at the wet spot on my side, made by the water running from the open bottle that I had dropped when the missile warning came. One bottle lost. I had two left.

The Red River had many sand bars and islands, most uninhabited. The high mud and silt content gives the river a red hue, hence the name. As we approached Tich Dong, the Red was wide and spread out, with a large island having some irrigation and planting towards its north end. Our target today was an S-2 missile assembly yard opposite this island.

The best approach to the target was along the riverbed with the significant terrain lying to the north. Further north, we could see the mountains on our right side, not a factor immediately, but a warning not to stray too far north.

Unfortunately for us, a road ran along the south side of the Red River with a concentration of mobile S-2 launchers located both north and south of a small village. There wouldn't be any chance of taking them out. We had to depend on speed and altitude to protect us. Coming up the river at 450 knots, the optimum speed to maintain bombing accuracy, we hoped that our low altitude and speed would make it difficult for the North Viet gunners to get a lock.

"Boss, the natives are restless this morning," my weapons officer called on the intercom. "I've got a string of hostiles along the river. They're getting an intermittent lock, but we should be too low for them to hit." This did not mean we were home free. The anti-aircraft batteries would score a few hits simply by filling the air with lead.

The S-2 missile system, used by the foe, operated on active radar homing. This meant when they acquired an active radar lock, they could fire with a reasonable chance of hitting the target as long as they maintained the radar lock. The good side for us was, with the use of this lock we received a signal that told us exactly where their radar and missile was located. It's always nice to know what hit you.

On the second run, we shifted our path to the south side of the river hoping to force the enemy to realign his guns and give us time to make our last run. The problem was we would now be vulnerable on the departure.

During the next twenty minutes, the sky was full of planes and missiles with more than half of them intent on doing me and mine harm. Sometime during the melee, someone on the ground got lucky, and we were hit, causing my flight controls to get sticky and the hydraulic fluid to stream down the side of the fuselage. While not a direct hit that would have finished us, it was enough to do damage. Looking down to my right I saw my enunciator panel lit up like a Christmas tree with more blinking lights than I could cope with. Shutting down as much non-essential equipment as I felt feasible, I re-evaluated the warning lights and decided we could stay airborne, at least for a while.

Air refueling was a key element of these missions since the amount of fuel burned during aerial combat was prodigious. After a few minutes in afterburner, the fuel supply was seriously degraded. The saying was the only time you can have too much fuel is if you are on fire. Today I had used up enough fuel to delight a bunch of Arab sheiks.

Air refueling required precise control of the airplane

and this was impossible in our present condition. The loss of the main hydraulic system rendered the flight controls to sluggish movements, much too slow and imprecise for air refueling. With insufficient fuel to make it to our recovery airfield, we would run out of airspeed, altitude, and ideas, all at the same time. The rotten part is this would all happen over hostile territory.

We would have to eject somewhere in the jungle. Tiger Two confirmed this to me in a solemn voice as we joined up, heading for a point called Thud Ridge. "Boss, you're spraying hydraulic fluid all over the native population. How do the controls feel?"

"Sloppy. I'm low on fuel, so you must be low also. It's time for you to head for the refueling point."

"Right, I'm breaking off. There are two Spads coming your way and Air Rescue has launched a Jolly Green Giant. Watch your six, big guy." Yeah, watch my six. Here I am about to go into the hostile jungle and he's telling me to be careful.

With a lonely, empty feeling in the pit of my stomach, I watched my wingman turn and pull away, climbing to refueling altitude. Keying my intercom mic, I said, "Well, Rusty, it's just me and you, baby."

"Not quite, I've got radio contact with the 'Spads' and they've picked out a nice soft spot for us with a river view. Also the helicopter is airborne, and they say they'll meet us over the ridge."

"Right, I'm sure looking forward to a ride in a chopper."

Looking at the problem we were facing I found it was by no means certain we would even make the ridge. We had lost too much hydraulic fluid, the flight controls were becoming more sluggish, and all good sense told me we had to eject before I lost control of the bird. "Rusty, how far do you estimate to the ridge?"

"If we make that cloud layer ahead we'll be past the ridge. Can you hold her together that far?"

"We are on fumes, my friend. Let us pray."

Shoving my hand into my pocket groping around the harness and shoulder straps, I pulled out my next to last bottle of water, and raising my visor and lowering the oxygen mask, I downed the thoroughly melted ice water. One bottle left.

The A-1 Sky Raider known by the Air Force as the 'Spad' was the perfect airplane for a search and rescue mission. Once a pilot in trouble saw the 'Spad', he knew he had a chance for survival. The 'Spad' specialized in ground support. The older, piston-driven fighter could fly low and slow, getting down in the treetops and providing protection for the rescue helicopters. This protection, holding any enemy forces at bay, gave the defenseless rescue bird the opportunity to pull the stranded crewmen out of the jungle in quick time.

The objective was to make the escarpment named Thud Ridge. The F-105 Thunder chief pilots, who had first flown the bombing missions into the north, named the ridge after the Republic F-105 airplane, which they called the 'Thud'. Making the ridge before ejecting would put us in Laos, supposedly neutral territory, and improve our chances of rescue.

Neutral in southeast Asia is a dubious word at best, and always suspect. This supposedly safe haven would better enable the Air Rescue helicopter from Nakhom Phanom, Thailand, to pick us up in the dense jungle of Laos. A jungle pick up such as this was extremely dangerous to the Pararescue men who would drop down into the dense jungle and make the rescue. As they hung from cables below the rescue helicopter, they were completely exposed to ground fire and defenseless to do anything about it. Maybe this explains why they were the most decorated people in the combat zone.

With luck and a lot of credit to the McDonnell Aircraft Company, we made it past the ridge to the banks of the Mekong River. Our fuel supply was now down to fumes and wishes, and I knew it was time to leave the airplane while I still had a measure of control.

"Okay, buddy." I called over the intercom radio to Rusty in the back seat. "It's time to get out of here."

"I'm set. My momma told me to never fly with

someone braver than I was, and I get hooked up with you. Okay, I'm ready."

Rolling the wings level, I looked to the right where one of the A-1 'Spads' was flying in close proximity to my right wing. Signaling with my hand, I announce on the command radio, "We are ejecting now. Keep us in sight."

"You got it, Tiger."

Reaching between my legs, I pulled the ejection lanyard blowing the canopy with a bang and a swirl of wind. The Martin-Baker seat came out with a thunderous roar, flipping me over backwards with the world slowly spinning around my visor.

The jolt of the ejection had not subsided when the parachute jerked the harness tight, binding my crotch and pulling my shoulders upward. Almost instantly, my left leg hit a tree sending pain through my body like an electric shock. The parachute canopy caught in the tree tops, swinging me crashing back into the tree trunk for the second time, adding insult to injury.

Ejecting at a low level usually meant the two of us would land close together. Rusty must have come down somewhere nearby, but from my lofty position hanging from a tree like one of Charlie Brown's kites, I couldn't see him. Looking up, once I had my helmet off, I spotted first one 'Spad, than the other crossing my patch of sky. I could not see the rescue chopper.

My first thought—hanging there in the trees—was how would I tell Janey about this without adding to the fear and worry she already had.

Thinking my leg might be broken, I was trying to figure out how I would get out of this mess when down through the trees a man dropped right beside me. The Pararescue man riding on an anchor-looking device hooked to a cable had me free of my harness and rising into the sky before I had further chance to react to my predicament.

"Did you get my weapons officer?" I kept asking desperately.

"Take it easy, sir. We'll have you in the chopper in just

a moment."

As we rose to the level of the helicopter floor, I saw Rusty leaning against the bulkhead and smiling the silliest smile I had ever seen.

The Pararescue Sergeant pulled me in the door of the Jolly Green Giant helicopter, and as I spread out on the floor of the chopper, he offered me a drink of water. Smiling, I declined and pulled out my last small pink Valentine bottle with its little heart boldly emblazoned on the side, now full of lukewarm water, saying, "No, thanks. I have my own, and I did, the sweetest water that had ever flowed.

## Author's Bio: Aubry Johnson

Aubry Johnson is retired from the United States Air Force and is a commercial pilot with over 25,000 hours of flying experience. He has written several articles that have appeared in Air Force magazines, and other aviation publications. Recently, a short story *Ice Cubes* appeared in **Harvest Magazine**. He created and wrote the curriculum for the U.S. Air Force Instructor Pilots School. Johnson, writing as Randolph Tower, has co-authored two novels; Ice and One Last Sin.

## Love Grows

by:  Cathleen Thompson

Wonder of you
For all that you do
Grateful each day
Loving embrace

Filling days
With your wisdom
Joy of laughter
Security of hugs

Eliminates fears
Warms my heart
Know we will never part

Love grows deeper
Love grows stronger
As time grows longer.

## I Never Said Goodbye

by:  Barbara M. Hodges

"Damn, Nick, you can send in your column from anywhere.  This is my chance.  It might not happen again." Josie turned, glared through the rain-splotched window and across the endless expanse of gray sea broken up only by the wind-whipped white caps.

"You should have talked to me before you accepted it," Nick said.

"I didn't think there'd be a problem.  We've been talking about moving to San Francisco for months."

"No, Josie, *you've* been talking.  I've been your audience."

"It's a new boutique.  I'll be the manager.  It's what I've been working toward."

"It's in San Francisco."

She turned to face him.  "That's a plus as far as I'm concerned."

"Why do you hate Cayucos?"

Josie sighed.  "I don't hate it.  I just want to see some place different."

"We both grew up here.  Our families live close by."

"San Francisco isn't on the other side of the world.  It's less than three hundred miles away."

"And what about Crystal?  I only have every other weekend with my daughter…"

"There are flights out of San Luis Obispo.  You can be here, or she can be there in a couple of hours."

"She's too young to fly by herself.  She's…."

"Thirteen, Nick.  She's not a baby anymore."  Josie took a deep breath.  "Just think, Crystal can come and spend time with us in San Francisco.  She'd love it."  She walked to him and touched his arm.  "Please, let's give it a try.  We can always come back if it doesn't work out.  God knows Cayucos will still be here, just like it is.  Nothing ever changes."

He stepped back from her.  "I'll think about it."

"Nick..."

"I said I'd think about it, Josie." He turned and walked away.

"Where are you going?"

"For a walk on the beach."

"It's storming out there."

He looked over his shoulder. "I don't care. I love the ocean. You just don't get that, do you?"

Josie heard the door open and close. "No, I don't get it." The beach was nice in sunny weather. She enjoyed letting the rays warm her and it was okay to walk and look for sea glass and shells once in awhile, but Nick could spend an hour or more just staring across the waves, and he didn't care what kind of weather.

She glanced at the large wall calendar. February thirteenth. She had to be there at the new store by March first. Maybe she had been wrong about accepting the promotion without talking to Nick first. But I didn't think he'd give it a second thought. He knows this is what I've dreamed about.

With a frown Josie picked up the five valentines she hadn't addressed or mailed yet. They were to their parents, as well as Crystal. "Well, I can always deliver them in person. Santa Maria's only forty miles away." The phone rang. "Hello."

"Josie, is daddy there?"

"He's out walking, Crystal. Can I take a message?" Take a message? Jeez, I sound like someone's secretary, but it isn't any secret that she and I have, at best, a civil relationship.

"Have him call me, okay? I saw something cool I wanna talk to him about."

"I'll tell him. How's your mom?"

Daria had a flu bug that didn't want to go away.

"She's fine. Resting right now."

"Give her my best." Josie cringed at those words too.

"Yeah, sure." And Crystal hung up.

Daria, Josie and Nick had all gone to high school together. Daria and Nick had been the super couple, the super couple that got married right out of high school, with Crystal arriving seven months later. The marriage had lasted three years

Josie and Nick had connected when he'd come into the boutique where she worked to buy something for his mom._ He'd asked her out, they'd been married a year later. Josie smiled, ten years ago, tomorrow, on Valentine's Day. Where had the time gone?

Things were not always easy. At times her paycheck was the only money coming in. But she'd never let him give up on his dream, and when he did start selling his pieces, he sold every one. Now he wrote a syndicated column that came out in newspapers all over the United States. "And he can send them in from anywhere. It doesn't have to be Cayucos, California."

"Josie," Nick said from behind her.

She hadn't heard him come in. Her body tensed as she turned around.

He stared at her for a long moment before saying. "I've got to go to Paso Robles to do an interview. I'll stay the night. I've already booked the room."

"An interview? You haven't done interviews in years."

"I want to do this one."

"Why all night?"

He looked away from her. "I need time to think."

"Nick." At his sharp look she changed her words. "Crystal called. She wanted you to call her back."

He moved toward the doorway. "I'll call you both when I get there."

"I'm going out for awhile. "

"I'll call your cell phone."

She flushed. "The battery's dead."

"Josie, what good is a cell phone if you don't keep it charged?"

"I'll charge it right now. I just won't have it with me, okay?" Her voice sounded sullen, and she didn't care. Just who was the one taking off? "Tomorrow's Valentine's Day."

"I'll be back by one." He walked from the room.

Josie stood where she was as he packed, and then left

without another word. Tears filled her eyes as she heard the car start and back from the driveway. She blinked them away. "Does he even remember that tomorrow's our anniversary?"

She walked to the fireplace mantle and stared at the photographs lining it. Her parents. His parents. Crystal at different ages. Their wedding photo. "And all taken at the damn beach." Well, except their wedding photo. They'd been married inside a white pagoda high on a bluff, but even then the ocean spread below them. "I just need something different. Why can't he see that?"She'd lied about going out and her cell phone. Childish? Maybe? But it had felt good at the time.

Josie turned, crossed to the large window and jerked the drapes closed. She'd just have a glass of wine, maybe two, and watch a couple of those chick flicks Nick hated. Tomorrow would be better, after he'd had his thinking time. *What if he says no?* Josie shook her head. He won't. He knows how much this means to me. She walked toward the kitchen to pour a glass of wine.

*****

Josie glanced at the clock again. Two p.m. She'd expected Nick home an hour ago. She groaned and rubbed her forehead.

Nick had called when he got to Paso, but their conversation had been stilted. After she'd hung up, she'd finished the bottle of wine.

"Stupid, stupid, stupid," she muttered as she walked to the television and turned it on. The local news was broadcasting from Morro Bay, an interview with the captain of a boat getting ready to take a group on a special Valentine's Day cruise.

Her eyes filled and she turned away. "Well, happy anniversary to me." This time she let the tears fall as she walked toward the bedroom. What she needed was a nap. Maybe by then her wandering hubby would make it home.

It was five o'clock when she woke. Josie lay there and listened. The house was too quiet. Nick still wasn't home, but at least her headache was gone. She kicked the blankets off and stood. Just where was he? Her anger rising, she went downstairs to where she'd left her cell phone, and then frowned. It had been turned off. *I don't remember doing that.* She turned it on. No messages. It wasn't like Nick not to call if he was going to be late.

Josie walked past the computer, and then turned and back-tracked. The monitor showed her email page, but the screen was blank. *I could have sworn there was an email from Mom. When did I delete it?*

"That's it. No more wine for me."

She heard muffled voices from the living room and relief flooded through her. *Nick is home. Who is he talking to, and why didn't he wake me?*

"Nick, I'm sorry...." Her words trailed off as her heart sank. It was the television. She'd forgotten to turn it off. They were still broadcasting from Morro Bay, but this was different. *Oh, my God.* The boat taking the Valentine's Day cruise had been flipped by a rogue wave. Nineteen had drowned. "Those poor people."

The doorbell rang.

Josie went to the door, opened it.

Mike Reynolds and Talia Taylor stood there in their police uniforms. Josie's heartbeat went into overdrive. It was about Nick. She knew it in an instant.

"Josie," Talia said.

She gripped her hands together in front of her. "Hey, guys. Nice weather for February, huh? Nick's not here. Would you like some coffee, or something?"

"Josie," Mike repeated. "It's about Nick..."

"Yes, he's late getting home. But he'll be here any minute."

"No, he won't," Mike said.

Josie backed two steps into the house. "Yes, he will, Mike. Don't you tell me differently. He's..." She swallowed, unable to go on.

"Let's go inside. I'll give your mom and dad a call," Talia said.

Josie held up her hands, keeping them from entering the house as she shook her head. "I don't need my parents. Why would I?"

Mike grabbed her hands. "Nick's dead, Josie. He was on the Valentine's Day cruise at Morro Bay. He drowned."

The world receded from around her. "That's silly, Mike. Why would Nick be on a Valentine's Day cruise without me?" The words sounded hollow and seemed to come from someone else.

"Let's go in and sit down." He guided her into the house.

Josie began to shiver. "No, it wasn't him. You're mistaken." Behind her, she heard Talia talking on the phone.

"I saw him, Josie. It's Nick."

A moan came from her. "No. No. No." She jerked away, whirled to face the picture window. The sun flooded the ocean with a gold shimmer. "You took him from me. You jealous bitch," she screamed. Her vision grayed and she fell into blackness.

*****

*Three years later*

Josie leaned against the deck railing of her sister Becca's house. Below, the ocean waves glistened in the afternoon sun. White caps formed and rushed in to spread across the beach. At the horizon, the fog hung, a gray jagged line separating the blue of ocean and sky. With any luck it won't start ghosting inland for another three or four hours, leaving plenty of time to take Phoebe on a long walk.

Cayucos, California. What would my life have been like the past three years if I'd stayed here?

Josie touched the letter in the pocket of her denim jacket. It was from Daria Taylor. She and Crystal still lived in Santa Maria, not far from Nick's parents.

She had read the letter three times and still couldn't figure out why Nick's ex-wife wanted to see her.

Daria hadn't even come to Nick's memorial. Josie swallowed. Three years. I can't believe he's been gone for three years. Damn, Nick. Her fingernails dug into the wood of the railing. Who takes a Valentine's Day cruise without their wife? And on their tenth wedding anniversary.

In the weeks that followed his death, she had tried to put the pieces together. There hadn't been any answers. Nick had bought two tickets, but no one she'd talked to had seen him with anyone.

The captain said the only people he'd seen Nick speak to were an older couple, the Mitchells. They were from Houston, Texas. She'd tracked them down, called, they'd been polite, knew who she was, but had refused to speak to her about the cruise.

Josie stared out across the water. Rogue wave. Even now the words echoed in her head on the nights she paced the floor and waited for the sun to rise.

"Josie."

She turned to face her younger sister.

"There was a message on the answering machine from Ted and Evelyn. How did Nick's parents know you were going to be here?"

"I emailed them and gave them your home number. We're having dinner tomorrow night."

"Are you sure you don't mind house sitting? I know it's short notice, but Keith and I hardly ever get any time away."

"Becca, it's fine. I was coming to see Daria anyway. And with—you know."

Her sister nodded. "The anniversaries are the hardest to get through. And with it being on Valentine's Day…."

Becca's words were meant to be understanding, but Josie heard the impatience beneath them. It was a tone she'd heard a lot lately. None had come out and said it, but it was there—it's been three years—time to get over it and move on.

"Any idea why Daria wants to see you?"

"Not a clue."

Her sister raked fingers through her cropped, red hair. "Well, Petey's in the small bedroom with the door shut. Keith would kill me if his precious macaw escaped out the front door. Although...."

Josie faced the ocean to hide her smile. Petey, or Peter the Great, as Keith called him, had come home with Becca's softhearted husband two weeks ago after a co-worker had revealed his plan to take the bird to the humane society. Petey was a gorgeous scarlet macaw, but the bird and Becca had yet to reach an understanding about his salty language, although Josie didn't think the threatened bar of soap was the answer. It had never worked for their mother.

"I mean it," Becca said. "Petey can stay in that bedroom until we get back. He'll be fine."

"That's good. Phoebe likes to chase seagulls. I don't know how she'd behave with a bird in the house."

"You can bring her highness in now."

"I'll do that."

Josie walked down the flight of steps into the back yard. "Like your new rose," she called back to her sister.

"It's a peace rose. Keith brought it home the same day he did Petey."

Josie grinned as she crossed the yard and pulled the length of rope that released the gate's latch.

In the back of the Honda CRV, Phoebe let out a loud woof of annoyance on seeing Josie. "Hey, it's not all my fault."

She dropped the tailgate and reached to open Phoebe's crate.

The tri-color basset hound made no move to rise. "In full princess mode, I see."

She stroked Phoebe's brown head. "I'm betting it won't last long. You must have to pee."

With a disgusted snort, the basset hound stood and sauntered forward.

Josie picked up Phoebe's long body and set her down.

Without glancing her way, the basset hound pranced to the open back gate.

Josie grinned as she grabbed the box with the basset hound's food, blanket and toys.

She closed the gate behind her and checked twice to be sure it locked.

Phoebe began to explore the back yard as Josie trudged up the stairs.

In the guest room, she placed Phoebe's box in the corner, unpacked, hung her shirts in the closet and put everything else in the chest-of-drawers across the room. "That's it. It's walk time."

"We're heading to the beach," she called to her sister as she walked through the den.

"Careful on the steps. They could still be damp."

Josie looked down when she reached the deck railing. The beach was empty.

In the backyard Phoebe glanced up as Josie stopped beside her.

"Yep, it's time."

The basset hound led the way toward the gate.

*****

"Which way?" Josie said as she stepped into the soft sand.

Three sea gulls chose that moment to land at the tide line and the basset hound charged forward in full voice.

"Okay, that way."

Laughing, Josie followed.

"You showed them, didn't you?" she said as she caught up with Phoebe.

Josie looked up and down the stretch of beach. Not a person in sight, all the way to where the pier jutted out. "Let's go this way."

In the shadow of the pier she glanced at her watch. It was three hours until her meeting with Daria at Café Noir in Santa Maria. *I wonder why she doesn't want me to come to her house? Could it be Crystal?*

It had been two years since she'd seen Nick's daughter and that had been at the Von's supermarket in Morro Bay. Crystal had looked right at her, but if Josie hadn't called out the girl would have pretended to not see her.

Crystal had been with a tall, thin boy with pierced eyebrows, nose and lip. Hers and Crystal's brief conversation had been stilted, but it had been long enough for her to see the girl's huge pupils and to know the she was high. In the middle of the exchange, the boy had called, "Crystal, come." And the girl had obeyed like a well-trained dog. The meeting had left Josie uneasy, but the girl wasn't her daughter and with Nick gone....

Josie drew in a deep breath of salty air. "Phoebe, come." As the basset hound reached her, a wave receded, leaving behind a pale sand dollar. She stood, scooped it up. "I got it before the gulls did. You know what that means? Good luck for us." She brushed the sand from it and stuck it in her pocket.

"Josie."

She turned and lifted her hand to shade her eyes.

Becca stood on the deck, waving.

"They must want to get going. Come on, Phoebe."

*****

"You ready?"

Phoebe wiggled in excitement. Josie had thought of leaving her behind, but then had decided the basset hound would make a great excuse if the conversation with Daria became tedious.

Josie popped the back hatch of the CRV and lifted it. Phoebe placed her front paws on the edge, and Josie hoisted the basset hound's backside. Before she backed from the driveway, she checked again to make sure she had the extra key and the garage door opener.

Tourists clogged Highway 1. She found even more traffic when she merged onto 101. Cars either zoomed in the fast lane, or crawled in the slow. It made the forty mile drive to Santa Maria, seem like a hundred.

I still don't see why Daria couldn't have at least met me

halfway in San Luis Obispo. A BMW swerved in front of Josie. She swore beneath her breath and inwardly repeated the new mantra she had adopted on New Year's Day. "Remember, they're people and not just jerks in your way." And as usual, it didn't help.

Josie saw the Stowell exit and took it with relief. Ten minutes later she spied Café Noir and slid into a parking slot.

Just inside the restaurant's door Daria sat at a small white table almost hidden by a large, split-leaf philodendron. Daria stared into space, looking lost in thought, so Josie took a few minutes to give Nick's first wife a quick look over What she saw made her frown.

The jeans and *Old Navy* sweatshirt were okay. It was the bright pink turban wrapped around Daria's head that caused unease to crawl down Josie's spine and then lurch upward to settle in her stomach.

She walked to the table.

Daria looked up. A slash of pink lipstick, the same hue as the turban, was the only color in her too thin face.

"Hey, long time no see. Let me grab a latte and we'll catch up."

They chatted about Cayucos, the weather and Zac Efron. It seemed Daria knew someone, who knew someone, who worked with his dad at P.G. and E.

"Is Crystal into him?"

Daria frowned. "No."

"How is she?"

"She's sixteen. What do you think? I've suddenly grown stupid." Daria shrugged, but Josie saw her body stiffen. "You haven't asked why we weren't at Nick's memorial service."

"No, I haven't."

"I was in the middle of chemo. My immune system was compromised and I couldn't be with so many people." She looked away from Josie. "Crystal refused to go. She had a hard time dealing with her dad's death."

"Did she tell you we ran into each other at Von's in Morro Bay a couple of years back?"

Daria shook her head.

"She was with some boy, and I think she was high."

"She probably was. It's the way she's chosen to get through things." Daria's words were delivered in a monotone.

*I'm going to regret this. She's not my daughter.* But the words came from her anyway. "What are you doing about it?"

Daria stared into Josie's eyes. "Doing? Nothing. Crystal still needs time. She's a bright girl. She'll see she's not helping herself."

"Daria, she's sixteen. Doing drugs and God knows what else. Nick would never have—"

"Nick's dead."

"But you're not."

Daria smiled ruefully. "Not yet, but I will be, and soon."

Josie looked away. She'd known it was coming. "Cancer?"

"It came back. I've got tumors in my head and liver."

"But the chemo—"

"Not this time."

Josie swallowed. "How long?"

Daria stared straight ahead. "A month? A week? They don't know."

"What about Crystal?"

"We've talked. I've told her, but she doesn't hear." Daria looked at Josie, reached to touch her hand. "You know my parents are dead. Crystal will be alone after I'm gone."

"There's Nick's folks. They love her," Josie said.

"Evelyn and Ted are too old to handle a confused sixteen year old girl."

"There's no one else. Aunts? Uncles?"

"It's been Crystal and me for the past three years."

Josie took a drink of coffee. "That's tough. What are you going to do?"

"I want Crystal to live with you."

Josie stared at her. She couldn't have heard right. "Me? Are you nuts? Crystal and I don't even like each other."

"You're a strong woman. You can handle her. She won't always be like this... it's Nick's death, and now my cancer." She touched her pink turban. "You could get her into therapy...."

"Did you get her help?"

Daria frowned. "I tried. She wouldn't go, and don't look at me like that. The time didn't seem right to try to force her... and what good would it have done if she wouldn't talk about anything?"

"Where's Crystal right now?"

"I don't know. She didn't come home last night. She must have slept over at Carson's."

"You don't know?"

Daria's lips thinned. "Don't judge me, Josie. You don't know what this is like." She looked away. "It was a bad night... the pain... I took some extra meds. I didn't realize Crystal hadn't come home until this morning."

Josie took a deep breath. "When was the last time you saw your daughter?"

"We went to the mall yesterday and caught a movie." Daria smiled. "That's when we get along best. When we're being friends."

"But you're not her friend, you're her mom. Sometimes—"

"What do you know about being a mother," Daria snapped.

Josie sat back in her chair. "Nothing. So why are you asking me to do this?"

"Who else is there, Josie? Who else? You loved Nick. Nick's a part of her. You can love Crystal, too. What do you think Nick would want?"

Josie felt panic tighten the wall of her stomach. "That isn't fair."

Daria's laugh was bitter. "Life isn't always fair." She pushed back her chair. "Think about it. I've already set everything up with my lawyer." Standing she looked at Josie. "Just don't take too long, okay?"

Josie nodded and then lowered her eyes to her coffee

cup.

*****

Josie turned into the driveway and thumbed the garage door opener. She pulled the CRV into the garage, switched off the engine and laid her head against the steering wheel. She was back at Becca's and didn't recall one minute of the drive. She remembered leaving Café Noir, soothing an irritated Phoebe and getting in the car. Everything else was a blur.

Josie shook her head. *Crystal live with me?* It will never work. *What do I know about teenagers?* And not just a regular teenager, but one with major problems.

Phoebe whined. "Okay, we're getting out." She exited the CRV, went around to the hatch, popped it open and hoisted Phoebe to the floor. "It's crazy, Phoebe. There has to be a better solution." The basset hound turned and walked to the door leading inside.

All was quiet inside for about thirty seconds, then, "Son-of-a-bitch. Son-of-a-bitch," came shrilly from the bedroom where Petey was.

Barking, Phoebe ran to the door.

Josie pointed at the basset hound. "You're not getting in there, so just pipe down. Maybe tomorrow we'll see about an introduction." She tapped on the door. "Petey, you hush it up. You're fine."

"Son-of-a-bitch. Son-of-a-bitch," was the reply.

Josie couldn't help laughing as she turned away. "Come on, I could use a glass of iced tea." Her stomach growled and she glanced at her watch. "Forget the tea. It's time to start dinner."

Josie thoughts turned to Daria's words as she put a chicken breast in the oven to bake and removed salad fixings from the refrigerator.

She shook her head. *I leave the house before nine and sometimes don't get home until after seven. Sure, Janie's boy comes at four to check on Phoebe and give her a walk, but I can't do that with Crystal.*

*I work every weekend, but Kelly would love a few more hours and there's the spare bedroom. I can move my computer...* Josie stopped the knife in mid-chop. *God. What am I thinking? Nick was always the peacemaker. Without him... no, it just won't work.*

She added tomatoes to the salad and then placed it in the refrigerator. "Come on, Phoebe. Let's go watch the sunset."

\*\*\*\*\*

A phone call reprieved Josie from *American Idol* and a screeching rendition of *Unchained Melody*. Grimacing, she moved to the phone. "Hello."

"Josie."

It took her a moment to recognize the voice of Nick's mother. "Evelyn?"

"Something's happened..." Evelyn's voice faded away.

"Josie." This time it was Ted, Nick's dad.

"What's going on? What's happened?" Josie's knees went weak, and she wobbled to a kitchen chair and sat down.

"It's Daria. She's dead," Ted said.

"What? I just saw her today, we had coffee."

"Crystal found her. She left two notes."

"Crystal left two notes?" Her words sounded as though they were being filtered through thick cotton.

"No. Josie, honey, listen. I know this is a shock. Daria left two notes. It looks like she killed herself. There was a recently-filled prescription for morphine by her bed, and the bottle's empty."

"Crystal?"

"We're here with her."

"What can I do?"

"You need to come over here. Right now if you can. One of the notes is to you."

Daria Taylor lived in the southeastern part of Santa

Maria. Josie hadn't been there for a long time but found she still remembered the house number; and even if she forgotten, there could be no doubt which house was Daria's.

A Santa Maria Police Department cruiser sat in the driveway. Next to it, a van from the local mortuary was parked behind Evelyn and Ted's black Honda Prelude.

Josie stopped at the curb in front of the house.

The drive over had been unreal to her. She'd kept telling herself that Daria was dead, but it wouldn't sink in. The sight of the police car and the van made it all too real.

She turned off the engine, then sat and stared at the red stucco house with its tan trim. Warm light filtered through the closed blinds. With trembling hands she opened the car door and got out. Her knees shook as she took her first step toward the house.

On the porch, a wash of light from the sconce bathed cherry-colored geraniums. Someone had stuck a large, red heart saying 'Wishing all a happy Valentine's Day' in the middle of the plant.

Josie blinked back sudden tears. "Daria, why on Valentine's Day?" she whispered. "Nick, and now you. Did you think the day was already so screwed up it couldn't be worse?"

She took a deep breath and rang the doorbell.

Evelyn answered it. Her former mother-in-law's face was pale, her eyes wide. For a long moment she gripped Josie's hands without saying a word and then choked out. "Thank you for coming. I can't believe this is real. We knew about the cancer three years ago, but she never said it was back."

*I didn't know. I never knew about it at all.*

Evelyn turned.

Josie gathered her courage and followed her into the living-room.

She saw Ted right away. He was talking to a tall, thin, man with white hair and a concerned expression. Two police officers stood off to the side by the fireplace.

Evelyn walked to her husband and Josie followed. Ted

grabbed her right hand. "Josie, this Mister Collins, he's from the mortuary. Doctor Jenkins has released Daria…" His voice broke. "…to him. They're getting her now."

Unable to speak, Josie nodded. Behind her, she heard movement and Evelyn's face grew even paler. Steeling herself, she turned. Two men wheeled a gurney from the hallway. A white covering shrouded a form.

Oh, God.

Ted's hand gripped hers harder.

She swallowed and looked away. "Ted, where's Crystal?

Before he could answer her question, she saw the girl walking toward them down the hall. She's gotten taller. She must be close to six feet, Josie thought. And so thin.

Crystal wore a long red sweater and tight jeans. In the center of the sweater was a black heart. Inside the heart was a red circle with a slash cutting through it and below the heart were the words, *Love Stinks! Boycot Valentine's Day.* Her hair swept her shoulders, and she had colored it red. More black hearts decorated her ears.

Crystal said nothing as she stopped beside Evelyn. Josie watched her mother-in-law slide her arm around Crystal's waist. The girl stiffened, stepped away, and Evelyn's lips trembled.

The pungent odor of marijuana drifted to Josie. Was Crystal stoned when she came home? Or had she just been smoking?

Josie glanced at the police officers. The older one frowned as he stared at Crystal. *Oh God, please not right now.*

He took a step forward, and the younger officer touched his arm. They spoke quietly, with heads together. Then with another dark look in Crystal's direction, the older officer nodded.

The front door closed behind the gurney, and it was as if the living room heaved a sigh of release. The younger officer walked to Ted.

"We're sorry for your loss."

"Thank you."

"We'll be leaving now."

The older officer joined them. "Mr. Taylor, I'd keep a close watch on your granddaughter. Teenagers need a firm family connection."

Ted looked confused as he answered, "We'll make sure of it, officer."

Josie frowned as she watched Ted. He didn't have a clue what Crystal was into.

Mr. Collins from the mortuary left with the police officers.

As the door closed behind them, Josie exchanged a look with Ted and Evelyn.

"How's Phoebe?" Evelyn said too brightly.

"What? Oh, she's fine. I left her in the guest bedroom at my sisters."

Crystal crossed toward Josie, stopped in front of her with her hands on her hips. A sullen question came. "What's she doing here?" The girl's pupils were dilated and the close, cloying smell of marijuana made Josie cringe.

"The notes, Chrissie. One of them is for her." Evelyn sniffed. "What's that smell?"

"Patchouli oil, Grandma, one of my friends put some on me," Crystal said, staring hard into Josie's eyes, daring her to call her a liar.

*You little brat. Now's not the time. But you can be sure we are going to have a little chat.*

"Where are the notes?" Josie said.

Ted reached into his pants pocket. "Here." He handed them both to her.

"She doesn't need to see that one," Crystal snapped, reaching for it. "It didn't say it was for her."

With a sharp look at the girl, Josie stepped back.

"Now Chrissie, of course Daria would want Josie to know. They were friends. Why they met for coffee just this afternoon," Evelyn said as she placed her arm around Crystal's shoulders. "This is all so heart breaking. Let's go into the kitchen and I'll make you some hot chocolate."

Crystal twisted away. She glared at Josie. "You saw

my mom today? What did you say to her? Is that why she's dead? Did you tell her to just give up—that there wasn't any hope?"

"Crystal Dawn Taylor, that's quite enough," Ted said. "You don't speak to adults that way. Not under any circumstances."

Crystal's glare turned on him, then she lowered her gaze and wailed, "My mother's dead. What's going to happen to me now?"

The question sounded sincere, but Josie had seen the quick look of calculation before the wailing started. They we're so out of their league.

Both Evelyn and Ted reached for the girl.

"You'll come and live with us of course," Evelyn said.

While they crooned over Crystal, Josie walked to the other side of the room. She looked down at the two letters. One had her name on it, the other read *To All Those I Love*.

She frowned. Does that mean me? Maybe Crystal's right. But I need to know.

She opened the letter. The first words written were, *I'm sorry.* Josie's lips trembled as she read the letter.

> *I saw my doctor yesterday. She finally said the word terminal. I've known it of course, but to hear the word was a shock.*
>
> *I can't go on. The pain—I can't sleep—I can't eat. It's like teeth ripping bites out of me. To even dull it I'm taking triple the amount of morphine I was just days ago. And it's not going to get better—only worse.*
>
> *I don't know if I believe in an afterlife. But anything is better than this. And if there is something beyond now, then I won't be alone. I've been thinking*

*about taking control of what's left for me
to control; and after today, I'm at peace
with my decisions.*

Josie's heartbeat sped up. *She means after talking to
me, but I never said I would.* She read the rest of the letter.

*I have to do it tonight, while I
still have the pills to make it happen.*

The last lines were to Crystal.

*My daughter, I'll always love
you. This can't be really much of a
surprise. You, more then all others,
know how I've been. No matter what's
beyond, I feel in my heart I'll be
watching over you, since I've always felt
Nick watches over us.*

*Love always, Mom.*

Tears filled Josie's eyes. She blinked them away as she
picked up the letter addressed to her. Inside, written in bold
letters, were just two words. *Josie, please.*

Her knees buckled. She reached for the arm of the sofa
and collapsed onto it.

"Josie, are you okay?" Ted said. "What did Daria's
letter say?"

She looked up. Unable to speak, she held the single
sheet of notepaper out toward Ted. He moved to her, took it
from her trembling hand.

He frowned as he read the two words. "I don't
understand. What does she mean?"

"Read it to us, Ted," Evelyn said.

"Josie, please."

"No, you read it," Evelyn said sharply. "It's in your
hand."

"It's what Daria wrote, Evelyn. *Josie, please.*"

Evelyn looked at her. "Please what? What did Daria want you to do?"

"She wouldn't want anything from her," Crystal snapped. "It probably means please, just stay out of our lives."

Josie shook her head. "I—"

Ted pulled another letter from his pants pocket. "Maybe this will help."

"Ted," Evelyn questioned.

"Daria gave it to me a month ago. It's from her lawyer. When she died, I was to open it." His voice broke. "I just didn't think it would be this soon."

"Well, open it, dear. It must be about Crystal coming to live with us."

Ted unfolded the letter, read it.

"Well, what does it say?" Evelyn demanded, as she tapped her fingers against her thigh.

In silence, Ted stared at the single sheet of paper.

"Ted?" There was a hint of worry in Evelyn's tone.

He cleared his throat and looked at Josie. "It's about Crystal's guardianship. Daria's given it to Josie."

"What?" Evelyn surged to her feet. "That can't be right."

"No way," Crystal screamed. "I'm not ever living with her. I'll kill myself first."

"Chrissie," Evelyn cried. "Don't say that." She tried to draw the girl into an embrace, but Crystal twisted away.

"I mean it. How could I live with her? The sight of her makes me remember it over and over—"

"What, sweetie? What?"

"Dad's death." Crystal's words bordered on hysteria. "Seeing her every day—no, I'd rather die." The girl turned and ran from the room.

"Crystal," Evelyn called as she started after her.

Ted grabbed her arm. "Let her be for now."

"But—"

"We need to talk. Figure out what to do." He crossed to Josie. "Today, when you met for coffee, Daria spoke to you about this, right?"

"She asked me to take Crystal when she died."

Evelyn stared at her. "My, God. Did you know?"

"Know what?" Then she realized what Evelyn was asking. "Of course not. She said *when* she died." Josie closed her eyes. "I didn't even agree to do it."

"But, why not us?"

Josie opened her eyes and saw tears running down Evelyn's cheeks.

*How much do I say?*

"Daria felt raising a teenager would be too much for you."

"Crystal's our granddaughter, no blood relation to you. You were just her stepmother."

"Enough, Evelyn," Ted said quietly. "Daria must have had her reasons." He looked at Josie. "And you haven't said you'd do it. Have you?"

Evelyn's eyes brightened. "That's right. You haven't. If not, then it's us. Right?"

"Yes."

Josie looked from face to face. Crystal living with them, doing whatever she wants. They'll never be able to control her. Damn you, Daria.

"I'm honoring Daria's wish. Crystal will come to live with me."

Evelyn moaned, collapsed on the couch and buried her face in her hands. Ted walked to her and placed his hand on her shoulder.

Heartsick, Josie turned away.

In a few moments Evelyn stood. "I'm going to go check on our granddaughter."

Josie turned and watched as Evelyn walked from the room, without looking back.

"You'll be taking Crystal back to San Francisco?" Ted said.

"That's where I live." She faced him. "I'm sorry. I didn't ask for this."

"I know. It's just…"

48

Evelyn's scream stopped his words.

She came running back into the room. "Crystal's not there." She turned and glared at Josie. "This is all you fault. If anything happens to her—"

"Stop it, Evelyn. Crystal's had a shock. She isn't thinking straight. She just needs some time—"

"Time?" Josie said. "For a sixteen-year-old kid?" She moved toward the door. "Where would she go?"

Evelyn and Ted looked at each other. Neither spoke.

Josie fought to keep her voice level as she asked, "Her boyfriend's place?"

"Crystal doesn't have a boyfriend." Ted sounded shocked.

Josie gave him a look of pity. "Girlfriends, then. Who are they?"

"Crystal never mentioned any." Evelyn's voice came, subdued and frightened. "We really don't know much about our granddaughter at all."

Josie hesitated in the doorway. "Call the police."

"The police?" Ted frowned. "Do you think that's the best move?"

"She isn't a criminal," Evelyn protested.

Josie spun to face them. "Crystal's a scared, messed-up kid. We need to find her fast, and we have no idea where to begin. Do you have a better suggestion?"

Evelyn sank down onto the couch. "Do you think she'd hurt herself?"

"Does Crystal have a special place—where she goes when she's upset?" Josie said.

Ted shook his head.

Josie clenched her hands into fists. "Come on. There must be something? What about when Nick was killed?"

"Morro Rock," Evelyn said.

Morro Rock. The thought made Josie's stomach lurch. *I haven't been there since Nick's death, and I used to love the place.* "You call the police. I'll look there." She turned back to the door.

"Josie." Evelyn's voice stopped her.

"Yes?"

"Bring her home safe. Please."

"Sure. Sure I will."

\*\*\*\*\*

Josie accelerated onto Highway 1. She'd driven the miles from Santa Maria to San Luis Obispo in record time, even for her.

*What will I do if she isn't at Morro Rock? I don't know anything about her friends.*

She raked her teeth across her lower lip. *Damn. If Crystal wants to stay lost, she probably will.*

She played over everything in her mind. It still didn't seem real. It was like a soap opera. "And I want to change the channel," she muttered.

She glanced at the clock in the dash, eleven thirty p.m. *It's still Valentine's Day.* Josie shook her head. "Will this damn day ever end?"

She took the Morro Bay exit.

Her stomach clenched as she passed the office where the bay cruises debarked.

The huge rock loomed above Morro Bay, a darker shadow, the stars, dots of light surrounding it. Her eyes had quickly passed over it a thousand times since Nick's death, but now she really looked at it and her insides calmed. *It's just a rock, nothing sinister.*

She turned left onto the road that circled it.

Mounded rocks lined the bay. There was only one car parked in the slanted spaces, a white Volkswagon.

*Is it Crystal's?*

She parked next to it, got out and walked over to the car.

The Volkswagon was empty. She tried the door handle. "Stupid. Stupid. It isn't even locked."

She found the registration in the glove box. The car did belong to Crystal Dawn Taylor.

Josie looked up and down the road, then across the

mounded rocks, toward the jetty.

"Crystal. I know you're out there."

No response came.

"I'm not going back. We have to talk."

Still silence.

"Fine. Then I guess I'm coming to you."

*And I hope I don't fall into the bay, or break my neck doing so.*

She grabbed a flashlight from the back of her car.

Josie paused at the bottom on the first rock. She waved the light across a well worn path.

*When I get a hold of her...which way?*

The smell of marijuana floated to her. "You stupid kid," she murmured. "What if I was a cop?"

Josie followed the path to a slanted rock and jumped onto it. She could see the glowing end of an inhaled joint and flashed her light in that direction. Crystal sat, cross-legged, on a huge, flat-topped boulder. The girl wore jeans, a green t-shirt and purple windbreaker.

*It can only be in the low fifties out here. She must be stoned out of her head, or she'd be freezing her butt off.*

Swearing beneath her breath, Josie made her way to the girl.

Crystal inhaled deeply, and stared across the dark water. She released the smoke. "Go away."

Josie sat down beside her. "You scared your grandparents."

"But not you, right?"

"Me, too."

Crystal held out the joint toward Josie.

"No thanks. I haven't touched the stuff since my senior year in high school."

"You've tried it?" Surprise and curiosity were in her voice.

"When we were in high school. Your mom and dad too." Josie looked toward the end of the jetty. "That's where the boat flipped over. Crystal, why here?"

"I come here a lot."

"To talk to Nick? Do you feel closer to him here?"

Her laugh came bitter and loud. "Not hardly. He'll never talk to me again."

"Crystal..."

"I come here to find the courage to kill myself." She laughed again. "You can see so far I haven't, but I thought tonight's the night. Things can't get any more screwed up." Crystal lifted the joint to her lips, inhaled and blew out the smoke. "But, I'm still here, aren't I?"

Josie thought of all the stupid things she could say. *You're so young. You've got your whole life ahead of you. Things will be better soon.* She opted for, "Why?"

"Good question. Maybe if Mom hadn't taken all of the morphine...I can't swim you know. I'd just have to jump in."

"Sounds cold and unpleasant, but that isn't what I meant and you know it. Why do you want to die?"

Crystal smothered the lit end of the joint with the toe of her tennis shoe and placed the stub in her jean pocket.

*Saving it for later, huh? Not an act of someone who plans to die.*

"It's better than having to live with you," Crystal said quietly, but with complete conviction, into the darkness.

The words stung and Josie looked away from her. "Why's that? You stayed with us before, when your dad was alive."

"We'd all be happier if I stayed with Grandma and Grandpa."

"No, you'd be happier, at least before you ended up in jail."

"I can run away, you know. You can't watch me all of the time."

"I don't want to be your jailer, but ask yourself why your mom chose me."

"She was out of her mind with pain," Crystal snapped. "She had to have been."

Josie sighed. "Daria loved you."

The girl scrambled to her feet; glared down at Josie. "Loved me? Then why did she leave me? Steal what time we had left?"

"I think she did that for you, too. Daria didn't want your last memories of her to be—"

"Yeah. Laying in the middle of her bed—dead—was better?" Crystal's voice broke and she turned her back on Josie.

"I—"

"Just shut up. I can't stand to hear you anymore." She pressed her hands against her ears for a moment and then let them fall to her side. "I can't stand to hear him."

"Him? Who are you talking about?"

"No. It's the only way. I guess I just needed you to be here." She whirled to face the dark water.

"Crystal?" Josie saw it in her face, the complete desperation.

*My, God!*

"No, you're not." She dove and tackled Crystal around the knees.

The girl pitched forward.

"Let go of me. Let go!" She tried to kick back, but Josie held on, her face pressed against the back of the girl's knees.

"Damn you, Josie. Damn you," Crystal screamed. "Just let me do it!"

"It's not going to happen."

"God. If you knew the truth, you'd just give me a shove." Shudders moved through Crystal's body. "I guess that's the way to let it play out. I have to tell you."

"Tell me what?"

"Let go of me. I'll tell you."

Josie hesitated, not sure about relaxing her grip.

"I'm not going to do it, at least not until you know."

Josie released her hold and sat back, but was ready to pounce again if Crystal made one move toward the edge.

Crystal sat on the rock, her back toward Josie. "The day before Dad died, you remember I called?"

"I remember."

"He called me from Paso."

Josie remained silent.

"I'd heard about the Valentine's Day cruise on the radio. I was excited and I wanted us to go. I told Dad. He was excited, too. Said it was a great idea, but then he had to leave for his appointment."

The girl shifted on the rock, rubbed her arms.

"You want another jacket? There's one in my car."

"No. In a few minutes it won't make a difference." She turned and stared out over the water. "After Dad hung up, I realized he hadn't told me when he'd pick me up, so we could go to Morro Bay for the cruise. I called him again, left a message on his cell phone, but he didn't call me back.

"The next day when he still hadn't called me, I decided to go to your place and wait for him. Cayucos is a lot closer to Morro Bay."

Josie felt unease crawl up her spine, and her shiver had nothing to do with the temperature. "You were at our house? You never said anything about being there."

"I didn't even know you were home."

"I was taking a nap."

"Your computer was on. You had email messages, and one of them was from Dad."

"My computer? I checked, there wasn't anything on it that afternoon."

"His email said he was sorry you'd had a fight. That you were right. The two of you could give San Francisco a try. That he hadn't forgotten your anniversary." Crystal turned to look at Josie with pain-filled eyes. "He told you all about the Valentine's Day Cruise. How he'd be waiting for you there. You. Not me."

Josie's stomach knotted. *Nick sent me an email about the cruise. He'd wanted me to meet him there.*

"I deleted it."

"You did what?" Josie's lips tightened as she waited for the answer.

"Dad had left six messages on your cell phone. He couldn't understand why you weren't at Morro Bay. He was angry when he left the last one. Pissed because you hadn't returned his calls. He said he had the tickets, so he was going on the cruise. That he needed some time to think about your marriage." She looked away. "I deleted all of them, erased your call history too.

"My God, Crystal!" He thought I deliberately didn't call him back! He went on that cruise thinking our marriage was in trouble? How could you do that to him...to us?"

Crystal looked away. "I was mad. Dad was supposed to take me. I was the one who told him about it. Instead he was going to take you." She stood. "I knew I'd be in trouble when he found out what I'd done, but I thought it was worth it." She turned and stared out across the water. "Josie," she whispered, "he wasn't supposed to die."

Josie hugged her stomach. *Well, now I know. Nick did remember our anniversary. He set up a romantic cruise for us. And I didn't show up.*

Her body trembled. She pulled her knees against her chest and laid her forehead upon them. *There was never another woman.* Tears filled her eyes and ran down her cheeks. *In my heart I've always known, but on those damn dark nights....*

"So you want to push me in now?" Crystal said.

Josie didn't look up. She couldn't.

*Crystal was just thirteen then. She didn't know the boat would capsize.*

Although her thoughts were logical, anger and frustration flooded through her.

*If I had known, I would have met him, but then maybe we both would have died. God, I just don't know.*

"Say something," Crystal demanded. "Say you hate me. Say how Dad must hate me, too." Josie just stared at her knees. "Damn it, Josie. Say anything. Don't just sit there."

She rubbed her cheeks against her knees and looked up. "Your dad would never hate you."

The girl went limp, like a rag doll. An anguished wail came from her, followed by body-shaking sobs.

Numb, Josie watched Crystal.

*I have my own pain. Why should I help her? If she hadn't...but, she's Nick's daughter. When I said I do to him, I knew she was part of the package. Get off your butt, Josie. You're the adult. Remember. She's just a screwed up kid.*

She crawled to Crystal, put her hands on the girl's trembling shoulders. "Your dad knows it was an accident. My mom always said that you love your kids no matter what."

"Does Daddy know? Does he really?" Crystal's words were punctuated with hiccups and sobs.

"I believe so."

"I have nightmares. The ship...the wave. Daddy's screaming at me, asking me why I did it."

"I've had some bad dreams myself."

"The drugs don't help," Crystal said. She sat up and hit the side of her head with the heel of her palm. "It's always right here."

Josie grabbed her hand. "Don't."

"How can I go on knowing it's my fault?"

"Crystal, you messed up, but the wave wasn't your fault. Sometimes things happen that don't make any sense." Josie looked across the girl's head toward the end of the jetty. "We just have to accept them, and somehow we go on." She stood and reached out her hand. "It's been a long day. Let's go home."

"I don't think I can drive."

"We'll go in my car. We'll come back for yours tomorrow."

Crystal looked at Josie's hand, then up into her face. "You still want me to come live with you?"

"It's what your mom wanted."

"But you? What do you want?"

She stared into the girl's eyes and felt her breath catch. *Why haven't I noticed before? They're just like Nick's, sherry colored with gold flecks. The sprinkling of freckles and thin nose are like his too. I haven't lost him entirely.* "I want you to come live with me. I think we need each other."

Crystal took the hand and let Josie pull her to her feet. They both stepped back, stared a long moment at each other, then they turned and walked toward Josie's car.

*One Year Later*

"Crystal, hurry up, or we're going to get caught in the Bay Bridge traffic."

"I'm coming. I've just got to grab my coat. I still can't figure why you'd make dinner reservations at Jack London Square at 5:30 on a Friday night."

"It was the only time slot available."

The doorbell rang. Josie swore beneath her breath and thought of just not answering, but her mother's voice would be guilt-tripping her the rest of the evening if she didn't.

She looked through the glass window. An elderly woman stood there. Forcing a polite smile, Josie opened the door. "Yes?"

"Mrs. Taylor? Mrs. Nick Taylor?"

"I'm sorry. I don't want to buy anything."

The woman smiled. "I'm not selling anything. I'm Irma Mitchell, from Houston, Texas. I'd like to speak to you about Nick."

Josie grabbed onto the doorjamb.

"Josie, what is it?" Crystal's voice came from behind her.

"Why now," she asked the woman. "It's been almost four years."

"May I come in?"

Josie turned toward Crystal. "Would you call and cancel those dinner reservations, please."

The girl looked over her shoulder. "Who is she?"

"Mrs. Mitchell. She was on the boat with your dad."

The blood left Crystal's cheeks. "I don't want to talk to her."

"You don't have to. Just cancel the reservations, okay?"

Crystal nodded as she backed from the door.

Josie turned back to Irma Mitchell.

"Is that Nick's daughter?"

"Yes. Please come in. May I get you some coffee? I will take only a minute to make some."

Irma walked inside. "No. I'm fine. I won't be long."

"Let's sit down." Josie led the way into her living room. She waited until Irma settled on an overstuffed chair, then perched on the edge of the matching sofa.

Irma glanced around the room. "Very nice." She waited for a moment and then looked toward the doorway. "Is Crystal joining us?"

"No… she has the flu."

Irma raised an eyebrow at the bald lie. "I know you are wondering why now? We wouldn't speak to you before…right after it happened."

Josie nodded.

"It was Henry, my husband" Irma smiled. "They call us the weaker sex, but that just isn't true. After the accident, he had nightmares. Very bad nightmares. He refused to talk to anyone about what had happened, even me. Henry wanted to forget it had ever occurred." She looked at Josie. "I honored my husband's wishes."

"Then why…?"

"Henry passed away a month ago."

"Oh. I'm sorry for your loss."

"It was his time. We had sixty-five, mostly good years together." She fluffed her white hair. "Have you ever stayed at the Seaside Motel in Cayucos?"

Her quick change of gears startled Josie. "A few times."

"Henry and I discovered the motel ten years ago. I love it there. I always try and stay in the Sunflower Surprise room. It's number ten. Have you seen it?"

"Nick and I had stayed in numbers nine and twelve. I don't remember their names."

"Number nine is the Cayucos Cottage. Henry and I stayed there before, too."

"Oh. Okay."

"Don't you love their garden, and it's so close to the beach and downtown."

"Mrs. Mitchell…"

"Oh, please call me Irma."

"Well then, Irma, is there something you want to tell me about Nick?"

She lifted her eyes to Josie's. "He saved my life, you know."

Josie swallowed. "No, I didn't know."

"Pushed me up onto some floating wood, told me to hold on, then swam away. To help someone else, I'm sure."

A knot formed in Josie's throat and she nodded.

"We talked a lot before it happened. I'm a good listener, and Nick, well Nick needed someone to talk to." She sat back and folded her hands in her lap. "Tell me, Josie, why didn't you come to take the cruise with him?"

Josie closed her eyes for a moment, then opened them and swallowed. "I didn't know he was there. I didn't get any of his messages."

Irma nodded. "I thought it must have been something like that."

"Was…was he very angry with me?"

"Angry? No. Hurt and confused, but not angry."

Josie felt tears coming and blinked her eyes.

"He loved you. Nick said he wasn't going to let your disagreement ruin your marriage."

"Oh, God." Josie let the tears flow.

"I just wanted you to know that." Irma stood. "I'll let myself out."

Josie nodded, unable to speak.

"Oh by the way. I'm in California to spread Henry's ashes. He wanted to be taken back to Cayucos. I'm going there today, to say a last goodbye to my Henry."

Josie sat where she was, staring down at her hands, even as she heard the door close.

Crystal came into the room. "I listened to everything she said." She sat on the couch beside Josie. "Thank you for not telling her it was me who erased all of Dad's messages."

Josie nodded.

"I brought you a tissue."

She took it and wiped at her cheeks.

"Dad saved that lady's life."

"Yes, he did." She looked into Crystal's pale face. "That was just like him, wasn't it?"

"I never said goodbye to Dad."

Josie's gaze shifted to the fireplace mantel and the Japanese-style urn sitting there. She had always planned to take Nick's ashes and give them to the ocean he so loved, but it would be four years, next Saturday, on Valentine's Day, and she still hadn't. "Me neither, but we will."

*****

They stood on the same rock in Morro Bay, the one on which Crystal had stood and threatened to kill herself. There were six of them, Josie, her mom and dad, Ted, Evelyn, and Crystal.

At first she had wanted it to be only herself and Crystal, but then decided to include both sets of parents.

The wind gusted every once in awhile, making them all shiver.

It was Crystal's suggestion they do it at sunset. Nick had always loved the moment when the rim of the sun touched the sea. Now, all eyes watched and waited.

Clutching the urn to her chest, Josie felt each of her heartbeats throb against the pale, gold-flecked, porcelain. *This is right, but it's almost like I'm losing him again.*

She felt a hand find hers and link fingers. Josie glanced across. It was Crystal. The girl leaned in close to Josie's ear. "He's not really in that urn. Dad's everywhere, especially here."

Josie blinked back tears as she nodded.

"It's time," Ted said.

She looked up. The sun just touched the sea.

She took a deep breath and removed the top from the urn. The wind seemed to hold its own breath for a moment and then blew gently around them and gusted seaward.

Josie stepped forward and dumped Nick's ashes over the side of the rock.

The wind picked them up and carried them across the

gray expanse of water.

Behind Josie, Evelyn began to sing *Amazing Grace.*

"No, Grandma," Crystal said. "This was dad's favorite song." And she began to sing the Beach Boy's, *Surfing Safari.*

Josie smiled. Nick had always been a huge Beach Boys fan.

Her parents and Ted's voices joined Crystal's, and after a shocked moment, Evelyn's did, too.

She listened to the off-key singing as she watched the sun sink into the ocean.

"Happy Anniversary, Nick," she whispered, "and goodbye."

She felt a hand take hers, give it a squeeze, and she squeezed back.

"Happy Valentine's Day." She turned to look at Crystal. The girl's eyes were shiny with tears, but she also smiled. "Come on, Josie. It's back to Grandma and Grandpa's for dinner, and then let's go home."

With fingers linked the two of them turned and walked from the bay.

## Author's Bio: Barbara M. Hodges

Barbara M. Hodges lives in Nipomo, California, a small town on the central coast. She shares her life with her husband Jeff and two basset hounds, Ophelia and Hamlet, as well as with Wallace a sassy orange tabby cat.

Barbara is the author or co-author of eight published novels; *The Blue Flame, The Emerald Dagger, The Silver Angel, Aftermath, A Spiral of Echoes* co-written with Maggie Pucillo, *Ice* and *One last Sin,* co-written with Randolph Tower and *Shadow Worlds* co-written with Darrell Bain.

When she is not writing she enjoys getting away in their motor home to local NASCAR races.

## A Valentine for Patsy

by: Spence Stimler

"I hate girls," Ralphy said as we sat on his front steps watching the new neighbors move in. It was one of those beautiful Indian summer days in late October 1931. Warm sun, no school since it was Saturday, and nobody bossing us around made it easy to just lie about.

My best friend, Ralphy, was again expressing his contempt for girls. I already knew he didn't like them, for I had heard him vent his feelings many times. I think I had similar feelings, but my attitude didn't begin to approach Ralphy's. It was almost mandatory for any self-respecting, seven-year-old boy in our town to say he didn't like girls. If any dared say he did like girls, he would be teased unmercifully and, in our way of thinking, risked being shunned for life.

Perhaps it was the circumstances of our family make-up that made the difference. I had two younger sisters, but they were still babies. I occasionally helped spoon feed my two-year-old sister, and when mom was busy with the baby, I was pressed into diaper changing service for the older one. This left me with a rather neutral attitude regarding the opposite sex.

Ralphy, on the other hand, had two older sisters. Susan was eight and Dorothy was much older. She was twelve. Both were assigned the almost impossible task of watching out for Ralphy, and I think that is where his dislike for girls originated. He felt he couldn't get away with anything, and Ralphy was the originator of almost all of the neighbor pranks. Why he was so concerned with his sisters was hard for me to understand because Ralphy didn't listen to either of them.

Dorothy was too mature to take much notice of him. However, Susan was not much bigger than Ralphy and physically in no position to make him mind. Her best weapon was to threaten him with telling their mom if he didn't behave.

I knew Ralphy didn't consider Susan had any control over him because only a few months ago he said, "Spence, have you ever taken down a girl's bloomers?"

"Of course," I lied. I hadn't really, but thought I could always fall back on changing my sister's diaper if pushed to prove I wasn't lying.

Ralphy was on to me. "I mean besides changing your sister's diaper."

"No," I shamefacedly admitted.

"Want to?"

"Sure," I said. I thought that was as far as it would go.

"C'mon." Ralphy headed into their house with me following wonderingly behind.

Ralphy's mom was shopping and only he and Susan were home. As we entered the house, Ralphy hollered, "Susan. Come here."

"What do you want?" she said as she approached us.

"Lift up your dress. I'm going to take down your bloomers."

I was flabbergasted and embarrassed. All of a sudden I wished I was someplace else. However Susan complied with Ralphy's demand and hiked her dress up to her waist exposing her pink bloomers. My familiarity with girl's underwear was confined to displays of intimate items in the Sears catalog. Mom allowed us to look at the catalog to wish for toys so the chance of observing anything else was brief at best.

Susan's bloomers must have been hand-me-downs from Dorothy because Ralphy was having a difficult time trying to undo the safety pin used to take up the slack in the waistband. As he fumbled, I kept wishing I hadn't agreed to his plan.

Susan must have tired of Ralphy's failure for she said, "You better stop, Ralphy, or I'll tell Mom."

Now I was really scared. If Susan told her mom, then she would tell mine and I would be in for a spanking. I think Ralphy got the message as well, for the lack of fear of his sister didn't extend to his mother.

"C'mon, Spence. Let's go back outside." I was already out the door and wondering why I had even agreed to his taking the bloomers off his sister in the first place.

\*\*\*\*\*

"Why are you telling me you hate girls again, Ralphy?"

"You know who's moving in next door?"

"Yeah. O'Rourke's."

"You know who they are?"

"I don't know much about them. I heard the folks talking, and they said they were moving from Eveleth. Dad said he went to school with Mr. O'Rourke."

"Well, guess what? They have only one kid. And you know what else? It's a girl, and the same age as us. Since they didn't move here when school began, my mom says I have to go with her Monday and introduce her to my friends. I hate girls."

As if on cue, the object of Ralphy's scorn appeared from around the corner of his house. This girl instantaneously enthralled me, even though I was only seven. She was just a little smaller, with dark, flashing eyes, and dark brown Shirley Temple ringlets. She was pretty as a picture, but it was her smile that captivated my heart. All of a sudden I knew I didn't hate girls.

She must have noticed my open-mouthed gaze. Holding out her hand, she approached me and said, "Hi, I'm Patsy. You must be Ralphy."

"No—no," I stammered as I stood and grasped her hand, shaking it gently. "I'm Spence. I live a couple of doors down the street in that yellow house." Ralphy could hate girls all he wanted, but I wanted her to know that I lived almost as close to her as Ralphy did. "This is Ralphy." I pointed to him without ever taking my eyes off her.

"Hi," Ralphy grunted. He didn't rise nor did he offer to shake her hand.

Overhearing the conversation, Ralphy's mom came onto the porch. "You must be Patricia. I'm so happy to meet you. Your mother has told me so much about you. You are a very pretty young lady."

"Thank you. Everybody calls me Patsy."

"Very well. Patsy it is. Have you met my son Ralph?"

"Yes, Ma'am. I just introduced myself to both Ralphy

and Spence."

Hearing her say my name and knowing that she remembered it sent my heart racing again.

"Patsy, I told your mother Ralph would go with you to school Monday and introduce you around, if you would like."

Ralphy groaned and whispered to me, "I told ya."

"That's okay. Ralphy won't have to. Mom wants to take me so she can meet the teacher."

Ralphy's sigh of relief was so loud it was like air escaping from a pierced balloon.

"Ralph, are you all right?" his mother said. Concern showed on her face.

"I'm just fine, Mom. "Now," he whispered aside to me.

*****

On Monday, Ralphy and I ran all the way to school and watched as Mrs. O'Rourke and Patsy entered the schoolhouse. Patsy waved to us and I waved back. Ralphy looked at me like I had lost my mind.

"Whatcha do that for?" he asked.

"Just being polite."

"Geez," was his muttered answer. "Next thing you'll be telling me you like girls."

"Hah, that'll be the day." However, I knew Patsy was somehow different. There was no way I could hate her.

Patsy's mom was seated next to the teacher when we entered the classroom. Patsy was sitting in a front row desk right ahead of Ralphy's desk. At first the teacher had us sit alphabetically. Perhaps she did this to better remember our names. As the school year progressed, she changed seat assignments and placed the ones having some difficulty learning in the front rows. Ralphy was now in the second seat and I knew it wouldn't be long before he made it to the head of his row. It wasn't that Ralphy was dumb. He just didn't take school seriously.

"Class, we have a new student with us. Her name is Patricia O'Rourke, and this is her mother, Mrs. O'Rourke," our teacher, Miss Adams, announced. "Patricia would you like to tell us a little bit about yourself?"

Patsy faced the class and the first thing she said was. "Everybody calls me Patsy. We just moved here from Eveleth and I'm seven years old. My birthday is July 5th."

Ralphy groaned because that was his birthday as well.

"We now live in a house next door to Ralphy and two houses up the street from Spence," she went on.

As our names were mentioned, all the kids looked at us. I felt embarrassed at the attention but nevertheless delighted at hearing Patsy mention my name. Ralphy, on the other hand, looked like he wished he were someplace else. On most occasions he loved to be the center of attention; that is, unless it involved his being associated with girls.

"I'm very happy to be here and meeting new friends. Thank you." Then she sat down and Miss Adams started clapping and we all joined in, even Ralphy.

It wasn't long before it was apparent that Patsy was one of the smartest students in our class, and she moved to the back of the room across the aisle from me. I was delighted as was Ralphy, but for different reasons.

Thanksgiving passed and as Christmas approached, we had our first snowfall. The snow was light and fluffy. We tried to make a snowman in our yard but couldn't get the snowflakes to stick together. We even had a hard time trying to make snowballs. When we tried to throw them, they were so soft all that came out of our hands were fluffs of snow. As the snow settled, we still couldn't make snowmen, but with a little packing we could make passable snowballs. Passable enough to allow us to run ahead of the kids as school let out for the day so we could pepper them with snowballs as they came down the street. We carefully chose our victims. We definitely weren't seeking anybody who would retaliate, so we limited our aims at girls. Bigger girls were our prime targets because they would mostly run and scream and not do anything to us. Sometimes, one would chase us; and if she caught us all her friends would join in, and we would get our faces washed with snow. When that happened, we would make false promises that we would never snowball them again.

We generally avoided snowballing little girls because they would cry and tell their mothers who in turn told our mothers. When that happened, we were not treated with a face washed in snow but instead to a rather warm backside.

We saw Patsy coming down the street with some of her new girl friends.

"I'm going to nail Patsy," Ralphy said.

I wished he wouldn't but didn't have the guts to tell him so. Ralphy let fly with a couple of snowballs in the general direction of the girls. They didn't amount to much and almost fell apart before they even came close. As Ralphy turned to make fresh ammunition, I saw Patsy had come prepared and had a snowball all ready. Before I could warn Ralphy, she let fly just as he turned and caught him flush in the face. I marveled at her audacity and was even more amazed at her aim. She had done something we only dreamed about—nail someone in the face.

Before we could counter attack they ran off and left me in open-faced awe and Ralphy sputtering with a very wet face. I knew then Patsy would be a tough one to get the best of.

Soon after it was determined that the ground was frozen and the snow was going to stay, an area was plowed and the snow banked up along the edges. Then one of the volunteer firemen fastened a hose to a nearby hydrant and flooded the area to freeze as the town skating rink. Not long after it was ready, Ralphy and I headed over skate for the first time this year. We both had clamp-on skates that no longer clamped. It was debatable what the bigger problem was: the worn soles of our shoes or too many attempts to tighten the clamps with pliers. The result led to the only solution possible and that was using fruit jar rubbers to secure the skates to our shoes. Even with all our innovations, we still had to use the two-point approach to skating—part on the inside of our shoe and part with the blade of the skate. Even so, we did manage to stagger around the rink and occasionally get in a game of hockey.

As we sat on a log trying to get our skates aligned with our feet, I heard Ralphy mutter, "Oh no. Look."

I glanced up and saw Patsy approaching, and over her shoulder was a pair of skates—not plain old clamp on skates, but honest to goodness shoe skates.

"Hi, guys. Going skating?"

"Wonder what she thinks we're going to do—go swimming," Ralphy whispered to me.

I'm sure Patsy heard him but pretended not to. She sat down on the other end of the log and proceeded to lace up her skates. I was green with envy but Ralphy pretended not to notice. He finally had his skates on and got to his feet. Ralphy got underway with a lunge and a few passable skating strokes. He managed to get to the other side of the rink without falling.

"Way to go, Ralphy," I yelled. After all it was our first time out this year.

By this time Patsy was ready and she stood and moved smoothly away with almost no effort. She sailed around the rink as graceful as a swan on a pond. I sat with mouth agape and Ralphy's eyes bugged out in astonishment. Patsy circled the rink, and as she came abreast, made a spin and stopped in front of me.

"Aren't you going to skate, Spence?"

All I could do was stare and finally blurted out, "Those are really nice skates. Where did you get them?"

"I won them in a skating contest in Eveleth."

"Won them? How long have you been skating?" My tongue was tied and all I could ask was stupid questions.

"I've been skating since I was four. Come on, let's skate."

I didn't know what to do. I was ashamed of my skating ability. Ralphy was pretty awkward, but I know I was even worse. Ralphy bailed us both out when I heard him yell as he fell, "Darn fruit jar rubbers. You can't depend on them. I hit that crack and the right one broke. I'm going home."

That was my cue. As Patsy turned to see what Ralphy was complaining about, I stretched one of the fruit jar rubbers around the edge of my skate and cut it. I couldn't have done a better job with a knife. "Darn," I complained. "Mine broke, too. I'll go with you, Ralphy."

"That's sure too bad, guys. I was hoping we could all skate together. Maybe when you get your skates fixed. Tomorrow? Okay?"

"Okay," I managed to reply. By this time Ralphy had both skates off, and together we headed for home without even telling Patsy goodbye.

When we were out of earshot I said, "Boy, Patsy can really skate, Ralphy."

"Yeah, I could too if I had nice shoe skates like she does. Besides she was just showing off. That's why I hate girls."

I laughed inwardly at his remark. Here was the showoff king of the whole county calling somebody else a showoff. Even with nice shoe skates, I knew neither of us could even come close to Patsy when it came to skating.

*****

A mid-December thaw saved us from further embarrassment. We expected thaws in January but never this early. By Christmas all the snow was gone, and our only worry was Santa's ability to make his rounds in a sled and no snow.

Christmas morning finally arrived, along with it a pair of roller skates for me. I was somewhat upset with Santa because the skates appeared to be old and had rust spots on them. I thought he hadn't covered them well and had let them get rusty on the way down from the North Pole. However, the day turned out to be very nice, so I decided to try out my new roller skates on the sidewalk in front of our house. I triumphantly skated down to Ralphy's just in time to see him come out of his house on a new pair of skates.

"Neat skates, Ralphy. Did you get them from Santa?"

"Nah. My folks bought them for me."

I thought how nice it would be if my folks could buy skates like that, but I knew it was impossible. We had too many kids, and Dad didn't make much money.

I didn't care, though. Dad had oiled these skates up and I could scoot along without any problem. Both Ralphy and I skated well on roller skates, probably because we were on four wheels instead of a single blade. We raced up and down the sidewalk; and as we passed Patsy's house, she came out on her skates. We weren't going to be intimidated by her like we were with the ice skates. Without a word, we sailed right on by and then discovered she was right behind us. She could handle roller skates as well as she could ice skates. We were hard pressed to keep ahead of her and were scarcely managing to do so when she hit a rough spot in front of her house. She flipped head over heels and landed on her butt, skinning her knee and tearing a hole in her pants. She got up right away and to my surprise didn't cry. Not even a whimper, even though I could see her knee bleeding. She brushed herself off and was prepared to skate again when her mother stepped out of the house.

"Patsy, are you all right? You're bleeding!"

"I'm okay, Mom. It's just a scratch."

"Scratch or not, you come in the house and let me put some iodine on it."

"Oh gee, Mom."

Turning to us she said, "Wait for me. I'll be right back."

"Okay, Patsy. We'll just be skating up and down the block."

As soon as she got inside, I said to Ralphy, "Patsy's really brave. She didn't cry or nothing."

"She will as soon as she gets that iodine on her. It really hurts."

I was sure Ralphy was thinking back to the summer before last when he stepped on a nail. The doctor cleaned his wound with iodine, and Ralphy could be heard screaming a mile away. Between the iodine and the tetanus shot, I couldn't figure out which one hurt him the worse. It must have been very painful.

"C'mon, Ralphy. Let's skate."

"Nah. I want to stay here and hear her scream."

I wasn't so keen on the idea of waiting but stuck alongside Ralphy. Ralphy listened intently for the first squeals of agony, but we heard nothing. The next thing we saw was Patsy coming out the front door ready to skate again.

"Betcha they didn't put iodine on," Ralphy said.

When Patsy skated up to us I asked, "Did your mom put iodine on?"

"Sure. Why?"

"Didn't it hurt?"

"It stung a little but really didn't hurt."

We skated a little longer. My admiration for Patsy went up a notch or two. She was as brave as any boy I knew, even Ralphy, and I told him so.

"I bet her mom didn't put iodine on. Bet it was mercurochrome."

I thought Patsy was telling the truth but decided to not argue with Ralphy. Actually, the first seeds of doubt were being sown regarding Ralphy's bravery. I was beginning to think he was a big baby when it came to hurts.

\*\*\*\*\*

The holiday season and celebrations were over. We settled into the monotonous rut of school work. As February approached, Miss Adams announced that we would again have a valentine box and that she would furnish us with red and green construction paper. We made our own valentines because most of us couldn't afford to buy them. She made a big box and covered it with red wrapping paper. On top was a big green bow and in the middle a slot to deposit our valentines. The plan was to take the paper home and make the valentines there. Then bring them to school and deposit them in the box. Of course, nobody was supposed to know who you sent the valentine to until they were drawn out of the box on Valentines Day. Needless to say, boys didn't send a valentine to a girl and vice versa. The exception was that boys did send a valentine to the teacher—at the insistence of their mothers. It was common for girls to send valentines to other girls which read *Be My Valentine.* Boy's usually read *Happy Valentine's Day.*

Names were signed, and sometimes we would try to get a boy in trouble by signing a girl's name. This tactic almost always failed because boys were so lousy at handwriting that nobody believed a girl sent it.

Valentine Day 1932 came and Miss Adams designated a girl named Jesse to pass out the valentine to each person whose name was on the top. Of course, Miss Adams got the most. Boys got the least, but the biggest surprise of all was a valentine for Ralphy and one for me which read *Be My Valentine,* and it was signed Patsy. She shyly looked at each of us with a big smile as Jesse read our names and the writing on the valentines. The girls giggled. The boys hooted and howled. Ralphy was furious. I was pleasantly embarrassed. We took a good bit of teasing for a few days but it was soon forgotten.

*****

It was late May when spring finally arrived. With it came kitten ball. We played in the dirt street in front of our houses. Ralphy had the only bat and ball, so he was captain of one team. I usually was captain of the other because Ralphy said so. Ownership of equipment carried many privileges. Ralphy flung the bat to me to decide who had first ups. I tried to catch it near the top, but it was difficult to do. I caught it with one hand, and Ralphy placed his hand on top of mine. This time I couldn't get three fingers on top of his hand without reaching the end of the bat. So Ralphy got to choose first and would be first up to bat.

Ralphy chose Lorraine and I chose Shirley. They were two girls older and bigger than any of us, and the best players even if they were girls. Next, Ralphy chose my brother Arm, and I chose our friend Dave. So it went until there were only two players left... Patsy and my little brother Dick. Dick had just turned five, and it was always understood that he would be on my team so I could take care of him. However, Ralphy chose Dick, and I was left with Patsy.

Since Ralphy's team was first up, I sent Patsy into the

outfield. The kitten ball was big and soft, and nobody could hit it very far, so I felt Patsy would be out of the way. I pitched to Ralphy, and after many disputed calls—we didn't have an umpire—he hit a ball back to me. I easily fielded it and tossed to Dave at first base. One out. Next up was Lorraine, and she spanked my first pitch high in the air and long toward Patsy in the outfield. To our surprise, she ran under the ball and actually caught it. She threw it back to me with a big smile on her face.

"Way to go, Patsy." I yelled.

"Lucky catch," Ralphy hollered.

Two out. Next up was my brother, Arm. I finally struck him out after tossing nearly twenty pitches. Nobody walked in our game.

We were up. I got to first base because Ralphy flubbed my ground ball. Then I got to second as Dave hit a ball beyond second base and Arm couldn't retrieve fast enough. Shirley was up next and struck out. My brother, Forrey, was up next and he struck out as well. My heart sank as I saw Patsy striding to the plate. I hoped Ralphy would treat her like he did Dick— toss a nice gentle ball so she could have a chance to hit it. Ralphy was of a different mind and wound up and threw the ball as hard as he could, hoping to strike her out. Patsy took a mighty cut and slammed Ralphy's pitch high and long—far over Dick's head. Patsy scooted to our first base, an elm tree next to our yard. Then she flew to second, a manhole cover in the middle of the street. Then on to third base... the telephone pole in Lorraine's yard. Finally she unnecessarily slid into home for Dick running as fast as his little legs would carry him hadn't quite reached the ball before she scored. We were ahead 3 to 0.

"Lucky hit," Ralphy said, but there wasn't much conviction in his voice. He was beginning to look at Patsy in a new light. "She wouldn't have gotten a home run if Dick wasn't playing out there."

"You wanted him instead of Patsy, Ralphy. Besides she would have gotten a home run even if you were playing in Dick's place."

Ralphy grumbled something unintelligible, and we went on to win the game.

From that time on, Dick was back on my team; and Ralphy chose Patsy first to be on his team.

*****

In the summer we learned of another of Patsy's talents. Mr. Jones loaded up the back of his cattle truck with ten of us kids for a trip to Lake Julia where my grandpa had a cottage. My dad and Mr. O'Rourke went along to help. We changed clothes in the basement of Grandpa's cottage. The girls changed first while we boys fussed about how long it took them. Some of the guys wanted to change in the bushes, but Dad and Mr. O'Rourke said no. In spite of our being last to change, Ralphy and I were first in the water, and after splashing each other, started to show off our swimming ability. We thought we were pretty good. As far as dog paddling went, I guess we were. We barely moved but weren't afraid to get our faces wet so that put us ahead of most of the other boys. We rarely went out deeper than our waists.

Suddenly, I noticed somebody swimming out farther in deep water. At first I thought it must be Mr. O'Rourke because I knew my dad couldn't swim very well. Mr. Jones was afraid of water and never went in, so I knew it wasn't him. I decided to put it out of my mind, and then I looked again and marveled at the swimmer who wasn't dog paddling but doing the crawl.

"Look, Ralphy. Isn't that Patsy?'

"Nah. It couldn't be. No girl can swim that good."

We knew it was Patsy when we heard her dad yell, "That's far enough Patsy. Don't go out any farther."

"Okay, Dad," she yelled back.

I was dumbfounded. She could not only swim but also holler back. If we tried to talk when we swam, all we got was a mouthful of water. That's why we never went out deeper than our waists. That way, so we could stand and cough until our throats cleared.

Patsy swam right up next to us and stood alongside with

a big smile on her face.

"I suppose you won a medal swimming," Ralphy sneered.

"Actually, I did," she answered.

"Where did you learn to swim like that, Patsy?" I was amazed at her abilities.

"Dad was janitor of the high school in Eveleth and they have an indoor pool. He taught me to swim after school. I can teach you how if you want me to."

"I can swim good enough," Ralphy said. He added, "I'm going to get out now. I've had enough."

I had always wanted to swim better so I said, "I'd like to swim like you do, Patsy."

"Okay. Now the first thing you have to do is learn how to kick your legs. Dad told me that is the biggest part of swimming."

I had my first swimming lesson, and it was from a girl. Patsy was very patient, and by the end of summer, I was swimming quite well. Not as good as Patsy, but a whole lot better than Ralphy.

Almost at summer's end Ralphy had me teach him what Patsy had taught me. Then, he quite reluctantly accepted instructions directly from her. Ralphy was slowly being dragged into the acceptance of girls as companions. Especially girls like Patsy.

*****

On the first day of school I hurried out of the house and ran down the street to meet Ralphy. We were going to be in the third grade. Ralphy had made it by the skin on his teeth. Our new teacher was Miss Moore. All the kids liked her but said she was very strict. She was the kind of teacher who suffered no nonsense; and if you didn't measure up, she flunked you and made you repeat the grade. Even if it meant she had to teach you again the next year. I thought Ralphy was going to be in a lot of trouble, so I wanted to enjoy being together with him in the same grade as long as I could.

As I approached Ralphy's house, I saw Patsy rush out of her house to meet me.

"Can I walk to school with you and Ralphy?"

I was delighted at the chance but had a concern about what Ralphy would say. Glancing over Patsy's shoulder, I saw Ralphy spying on us from behind the curtain in their window. I decided, *"The heck with Ralphy; I don't care what he or anybody else says I'm going to walk with her."*

"Sure, Patsy."

"Do you think Ralphy will care?"

"We'll soon find out. Here he is. Ralphy, Patsy is going to walk to school with us. Okay?"

"Okay, but I'm not going to carry her books."

"You're silly Ralphy. I'll carry my own books."

"Okay, but I'm not going to dilly-dally." He took off in a dead run and when I didn't run after him, Patsy looked pleased and gave me one of her beautiful smiles. I don't know why, but my knees felt weak when she smiled at me like that. I couldn't have run if I had wanted to.

When he got a block ahead, Ralphy turned. When he saw we weren't running after him, he waited till we caught up.

"Boy, you guys are really slow." I grinned and Patsy gave him a big smile. Ralphy wilted. Patsy had captured both of us.

As we approached the school grounds, all our gang was out in force to greet us.

"Spence has a girl friend," they taunted.

"Ralphy has a girl friend."

I was a bit embarrassed but not enough to say anything. Patsy strode proudly between us and Ralphy glared. He didn't say anything, but he looked each of our hecklers in the eye. They got the message. Ralphy was far from one of the biggest kids but his reputation for toughness was well known. None of the antagonists wanted to be the one to answer to Ralphy when he got him alone. Truth of the matter was that Patsy did have two boy friends.

\*\*\*\*\*

With the arrival of fall our thoughts turned to football. Because we didn't have equipment, we played touch football—again in the street. Patsy was out with us when her dad spotted her.

"Patsy, football isn't for ladies. C'mon up here on the porch. You can watch with me."

"Oh gee, Dad. I can play okay."

"I know you probably can, but someday you have to grow up to be a lady. Now is a good time to start."

She was disappointed. I was disappointed, and even Ralphy rued Patsy's dad's decision. Ralphy had by now accepted Patsy as a full and equal partner even if she was a girl. We both knew she would probably shine as a football player just as she did at everything else she tried.

\*\*\*\*\*

We enjoyed a beautiful fall with yet another long Indian summer. Patsy had been with us a year now, but in some ways it seemed like she had been here from the beginning. We walked to and from school with her, and in her quiet way she helped Ralphy with his homework. He didn't realize it, but I could see an improvement in his attitude toward school even though he still suffered poor grades. I was sure he would repeat third grade next year and was saddened to think of him not being in our class.

In December our small town was dealt a crushing blow in the form of a scarlet fever epidemic. It spread through school like wild fire. First one family and then another was stricken, and the health department posted yellow quarantine signs on their front and back doors.

On Monday, the week before we were to begin Christmas vacation, I woke up feeling ill. My throat was sore.

Mom noticed my lethargy. "Spencer, are you feeling all right?"

"I think I'm coming down with a cold, Mom." Seemed like we were always catching colds.

She felt my forehead. "You feel feverish. Let me look at your throat."

I opened my mouth and Mom moved me over to the light so she could see.

"Say ah," she said using a spoon to depress my tongue. She looked and moved the spoon around. "I think you might have scarlet fever, son. Here, let me take your temperature."

She shook the thermometer and put it in my mouth. After a few minutes she looked and said, "You are running a temperature. I'm going to have the doctor look at you. Armin and Forrest, get dressed but don't plan on going to school until after the doctor comes." Both of my brothers tried unsuccessfully to hide their delight. They were of the same mind as Ralphy when it came to school—something which they were forced to tolerate.

Mom called Dr. Donaldson who said he would be there right after stopping at O'Rourke's. He said their little girl seemed to be ailing and probably had scarlet fever.

When the doctor arrived, he checked me out and confirmed Mom's diagnosis. I had scarlet fever. "You know I'm also the county health officer, and I'll have to quarantine you for two weeks. Scarlet fever is very contagious."

Neither Arm nor Forrey could hide their glee. Because I had scarlet fever, they would get an extra week's vacation. Arm's elation lasted three days. I never did break out in much of a rash, but he more than made up for it. He was quite ill, and Mom was very worried. About the time Arm started to get better, Forrey caught the disease. Now we would be quarantined for three weeks.

Dad moved out of the house and stopped by every morning to see what mom needed so he could bring it to her on his way home. He stayed with his folks who lived in town. He also brought news of what was going on. It seemed that almost every family was down with the disease. Large ones like ours were hit the hardest because each new case meant a new start for the quarantine period. By the time the disease ran its course in our family, we were quarantined for six weeks.

It was February before I returned to school, and I raced

down the street to meet Patsy and Ralphy. Ralphy met me and I asked, "Where's Patsy?"

"She's still sick."

"I didn't know scarlet fever lasted this long."

"It's not scarlet fever. I think she has an ear infection. Mom said she was still running a high fever."

"I hope she gets okay soon."

"Me, too."

In school, Miss Moore welcomed all of us back. This was the first time that the class, except for Patsy, was full since before Christmas. Many of us had kept up with our schoolwork. In my case, Dad brought the assignments from Miss Moore, and Mom helped me. So most of us were up to date—Ralphy being the one exception. He took full advantage of his illness and true to form hadn't done one stitch of schoolwork.

The next Monday when I came downstairs for breakfast, I noticed Mom had a long face. She didn't hide her emotions easily. "Son," she said to me, "they took Patsy to the hospital in St Cloud last night. The doctor said she has a mastoid."

"What's a mastoid?"

"It's an infection behind the ear. It's very serious."

"She'll be okay, won't she?"

"We can only hope and pray."

When I passed the O'Rourke's house on the way to school, I didn't see any activity. Ralphy met me and said, "Did you hear that they took Patsy to the hospital last night?"

"Mom just told me."

"Mr. O'Rourke gave his house key to Dad so we could watch their place. They are going to stay in St. Cloud with Patsy."

Two days later we had a new snowfall and coming home from school, Ralphy and I enjoyed our favorite sport—peppering girls with snowballs. As we approached Ralphy's house, he saw his mother at the front door.

"Oh, oh," Ralphy said, "I wonder who told something on me now. Well, I guess I better go in and face the music."

He plodded up the steps and I ran on home.

Mom was waiting inside and one look at her face told me something was wrong. "I have bad news, son. Patsy passed away this morning."

I couldn't believe what she was saying. "You mean she died?"

"Yes. She was a very sick little girl."

I just stood there. I knew tears were forming in my eyes. I started to say something but all that came out was a squawk. I had a big lump in my throat and I couldn't swallow it away. Mom saw my anguish and held me in her arms. She sobbed and said, "It's okay to cry. It'll help if you do." I wanted to cry, but couldn't.

"Mom, I don't understand. Little kids aren't supposed to die—only old people."

She looked at me wonderingly.

"Oh, I don't mean old like you and Dad. I mean like Grandpa and Grandma. That's not what I mean, either. I'm confused."

"I understand what you mean, son. Patsy's in heaven with Jesus and she's happy."

I couldn't think of anything else to say, so I turned and looked out the window to the place where we had played so many games with Patsy. I tried to shut my mind. It hurt too much to think about her.

The next day in school, Miss Moore announced that Patsy's funeral would be the day after tomorrow at ten o'clock, and we would march over in a group to attend, so we should be dressed up. Patsy's family was Catholic, and the church was across from the school.

On the day of the funeral, I met Ralphy and we slogged our way to school angrily kicking any clod of snow or ice in our way. Ralphy and I had never been inside a Catholic church. Most of our friends were Catholic and they had told us of their ritual and it seemed very complicated to a couple of Presbyterian boys. We knew of such things as genuflecting and making the sign of the cross, but had no idea of how or when to do it.

"Ralphy, do you know what to do in the Catholic Church?"

"Nope. Mom said that Miss Moore is Catholic, and she'll tell us what to do."

In school Miss Moore said, "Class, we'll leave here at a quarter to ten. I'll lead the way and show you to your seats. For those who are not Catholic, all you have to do is stay seated. We will enter by a side aisle and I will lead you to our seats. When the service is over, we will pass by the coffin and leave by the center aisle."

Entering the church, I noticed an almost overpowering aroma of fresh flowers, and I wondered where they got fresh flowers in the middle of winter. I didn't see Patsy's casket until we were seated. As it turned out, I was on the center aisle and Ralphy was next to me. Our class took up two rows, and Miss Moore was directly behind me in the second row. Across the aisle, I saw Mrs. O'Rourke sobbing softly as Mr. O'Rourke held her close to him.

The service was in Latin and I didn't understand anything being said. Perhaps it was just as well, for I found myself not thinking of Patsy, but instead on the beauty of the sculptures—particularly in the altar area. Our church was very plain by comparison. Soon the service was over, and Miss Moore stood and beckoned us to follow her. She approached the coffin, genuflected, and made the sign of the cross. She rose and nodded to us. I approached the casket with Ralphy at my side. Neither of us knew what to do. As I stood there, all I could think of was Patsy and how she just couldn't be in that little container. I had never been sadder in my life; and in spite of my efforts, I couldn't prevent tears from running down my cheeks. I tried to wipe them away with the back of my hand. Ralphy was having trouble with his nose and wiped the sniffles with his sleeve. Neither of us has thought to bring a handkerchief.

Miss Moore didn't move and we stood sad and perplexed. Then I felt a hand on my shoulder. I looked up and saw Patsy's mom with her hands on both Ralphy's and my shoulders. She smiled the same gentle smile Patsy used to give us, gave us a gentle hug, and whispered, "Come with me."

With Ralphy and me on either side of her, she walked down the aisle to the back of the church. All our class followed behind us, and Miss Moore led us back across the street and into our classroom.

We hung our wraps in the cloak room and silently took our desks. All the girls showed evidence of crying and some were still sobbing. Even Miss Moore's eyes were red. We boys avoided looking at each other and hung our heads and studied the floor. Everybody was full of sorrow and depressed.

Miss Moore broke the spell and said, "Class, today is a very sad day for all of us. It is also Valentines Day. We will open the valentine box and pass them out. Then the class will be dismissed and you can go home early. Ralph, will you please be the one to hand out the valentines."

Ralphy rose from his seat and tore open the box. Reaching inside, he pulled out the first valentine. It was for Patsy.

"Pass all Patsy's valentines to me, and I'll collect them and take them to her parents," Miss Moore instructed.

The next valentine was for Patsy as was the following one. One by one the valentines for Patsy were placed on Miss Moore's desk. The last one was the biggest and was from Ralphy. He had pasted four pieces of red construction paper together and cut it in the shape of a heart. He held it up for all to see. It read:

*TO PATSY*
*BE MY VALENTINE*
*FROM*
*RALPHY*

Even though we had made the valentines before Patsy passed away, nobody had made one for anybody other than Patsy. I could feel Patsy looking down and smiling—happy to receive all the valentines and knowing we all loved her. Unknowingly, she had given us each a valentine. For Patsy knew that as nice as it was to be loved, it was far better to be the one who loved—the greatest of all valentines.

## Author's Bio: Spence Stimler

Spence Stimler retired from his vocation as an Electrical Engineer in 1982. He began to write in 1998 at the age of 75. Mister Stimler is the author of two books—both memoirs of his early life in Minnesota during the Great Depression.

The first; *No Silver Spoon* was published in 2004. His second book, *Adventures With Buddy* was published in 2006. In addition he has had numerous stories published in the magazine, *A New Day.* Spence Stimler lives in Santa Maria, California

## Prism of Long Love

by:  Cathleen Thompson

Twenty nine years of love.
Seems like yesterday we first met,
Liked you instantly.
Your blue eyes took my breath away.

Your mind a prism of creative knowledge,
Got lost in a conversation
that fed my soul.
Getting to know you was a treat
for all the senses.

Learning about you still brightens my day.
We've gone though many trials
making our love grow deeper,
Hope for many more years to flourish
together in love forever.

## If I Loved You

by: Thelma Flory Walker

It was noon Saturday when Ann arrived by cab at the door of the *Time Out*, a dingy café every bit as rundown as the rest of the old, gray neighborhood near downtown Detroit. Joe had mentioned the place a time or two long ago, at least it seemed long ago now, that summer of 1987. He'd described it as a gathering place where neighborhood people got together.

Another women might have turned back at this point, but hadn't she come all this way? Wasn't this her destination, this place that was her only link to Joe?

She squinted in the sunlight at the metallic glint in the old gray dust. Joe's neighborhood. Would he still be here? Suppose he had gone. Would it matter? The sudden pain she felt told her it would. If he were gone, well then, he'd be gone.

Ann walked through that door of the *Time Out* with its peeling once-white paint and directly into Joe's silent, waiting presence. She instantly felt the grip of those familiar black eyes.

"Oh, Joe," she said.

He did not smile, nor did he speak, his handsome features unreadable as he cupped her elbow in the palm of his hand and steered her to a small round table in the sparsely peopled room.

"What are you doing here?" he demanded as he sat down opposite her.

His voice was as she remembered it, soft as velvet.

"Why did you come? Why now? Are you slumming, gathering off-color material for some expose?"

Ann was bewildered by his gruff manner, "I came all the way from upstate New York just to find you."

"Should I be flattered?"

"No. Just civil."

"Civil? It's been four years. You said you'd write."

"I was abroad."

"Oh, yeah, I forgot. That's where rich kids go after

85

graduation."

"So? Wouldn't you?"

"Sure, but the Europe I'd see would be worlds apart from what you went for. I'd see the inner cities, the slums, where the real living goes on." He leaned toward her. "So, why did you come?"

"Well, not to fight. I came to see how a friend was doing, but I guess that was a mistake." She got to her feet.

"Okay. Okay." He caught her wrist as he stood up. "So you came to see me? I'm glad, glad to see you. Really. I'm sorry. I'm treating you badly. Please sit down. Please. I thought you'd forgotten me. I looked for you every day—for a letter, a card, or *something* until I was sure you wouldn't come. Then, all at once, here you are."

She freed her hand and settled back in the chair, reluctant to admit she understood.

"So, tell me," Joe said. "What have you been doing since you've been back? Are you working? Married?"

"I'm between assignments. And no, I'm not married."

"In other words, you haven't found a job yet, or the right man." He sat back, an arm stretched casually across the table and the other around the back of his chair,

"Well, not one I want. What are you doing?"

"Not married." He answered that unspoken question first, "I have a law practice. And I'm running for the United States Congress."

"Really? Well, you didn't waste any time, did you?" She tried to appear unimpressed, when actually she was stunned.

"No. There's no time to waste. I'm already thirty-four. And I've only just begun. I have some good backers and I have two good people working for me. Would you like to meet them? How long are you going to be around?"

"Today."

Joe suddenly stood. "I have to pick something up right now, want to come along?"

"What?"

"I have to go. Do you want to come along? It'll give us

a chance to catch up."

She should leave. She knew it. This could go nowhere and she'd seen him. Ann stood too."Why not."

Ann hoped it would be like old-times, the two of them walking together, not intimately, just friends, the way it was on campus.

But it wasn't the same. Joe's silent reserve created a pounding disturbance within her. Although he had always been quiet, it had never been intimidating -- combative. Today it was both those things.

They walked three blocks to an old, rehabilitated red brick mansion on Grand Boulevard. They mounted the crumbling cement steps. Joe pushed open the massive door with beveled glass window and Ann could see it was a library.

Inside, he led the way through the book-lined walls, to a special section where he ran his finger along a row of volumes, selected one, and withdrew it. He turned the book over in his hands a few times before holding it out to her.

She read the title, *How to Run a Campaign.*

"Would you like to read this?"

"Why ever would I want a book like that?

"You're not working. So, I was hoping you'd join my campaign. Work with me. Run things for me."

"Me? Run things for you? I don't know anything about campaigns. I don't even like politics."

"You don't have to. You can write. You could help," his chin jutted out, "I need you."

His look was like the touch of a live wire and she half laughed to ease the sudden spark she felt.

"You might need someone, but not me. What could I do?"

"I read everything you wrote for the University Press. You're good. You present the facts well and you're persuasive. I read your stuff even before I knew you," he paused, "So, how about it?"

"What kind of a job would that be for me? I'm a journalist. I need a job that leads somewhere."

"This wouldn't be a job. It would be a commitment."

The word hit her like a fist in the pit of her stomach. At school there had been no commitment.

She and Joe had graduated, and, like homing pigeons, each returned to his own loft. Socially incompatible relationships like theirs dissolved without question, if not without pain.

Shaking her head against the insanity of his offer, she turned away.

"How could I? How would it look, especially to my family? My father? I'm white and you're..."

"Black," he finished for her. "Is that it?"

"Yes. Of course that's it. What would people say? Besides, you might use me like father says you people do. Use me and then embarrass me about it later. A kind of black revenge."

He grabbed her arm and swung her around, his scowl like thunder.

"If you think I'm capable of that kind of deceit, we have nothing. You're going to tell me you don't trust me because I'm black? That you don't feel anything for me because I'm black?"

She pulled away from his grip. "I came here because we were friends. I do care about you -- as a friend. Isn't that enough?"

He turned away from her. "If you leave now, then what?"

"And if I stay?"

Joe turned, fixed her with his steady eyes. "You'd be with me."

Ann felt a painful knot in her throat. His words were a challenge, a challenge to the casual friendship they had maintained before graduation, a friendship held at bay by overly polite restraint. But this wasn't kids' stuff now. This wasn't a display of tolerance or defiance at school. This wasn't a show, making a brave, bold statement of accepting him as an equal. This was life. This was stepping forward in the eyes of the world, setting your compass.

If she turned away now…?

But if she stayed…?

"I'll take a look at it," she offered quietly as she reached for the book.

"Okay." He took her elbow again in his hand and motioned with the other toward the door. "It's early. Would you like to meet the others now? I'll drive you to your place later."

The others were Belle Johnson, a stylish young black woman with even features and tamed silky hair, and Ed Kiplinger, called Kip, who was, to Ann's surprise, a young white man, shy, but decidedly Madison Avenue.

Ann settled into the group and also into a sometimes stormy, often playful relationship with this dignified, aggressive, and ambitious black man, Joseph Tannerhill, lawyer and candidate for the United States Congress. Her one stipulation to him from the beginning of this new arrangement was that she remain in the background, out of public view and there be no show of sociality between them.

"I understand," he said, "You can disguise it any way you like."

"I don't mean that," she'd protested, knowing full well she'd meant exactly what he'd said.

"Please." Joe had put up his hand to halt any further discussion on the subject, "It's all right. I *do* understand."

In her letters home, Ann had said little about her work, only that she was writing speeches and arranging speaking engagements for a politician. After all, she was twenty-seven. She didn't need to justify her decisions to her family.

It was now spring of the following year and the staff was preparing for a trip to Memphis where Joe was invited to address the NAACP.

It was the day before they were to leave and Ann was at her desk in the large, unpretentious campaign headquarters, and Joe at his. Joe's desk was about twenty feet away near the windows, and hers against the wall.

The door opened and Ann looked up.

"Dad," she said, delighted and alarmed as she got up to great him.

"Hello, Ann," he said, "How are you?"

"I'm just fine Dad," she said as they embraced. "What are you doing in Michigan?"

"Oh, I had some business with the folks at GM and I thought it would be an excellent opportunity to see where you were working."

"Well, this is it." She waved her hand in a sweeping circle. "Why didn't you tell me you were coming?"

"I didn't know until this morning and you never did give us your office phone number. But I can't stay. Just thought we might have lunch together before I have to leave."

He glanced around, not seeming to notice the dark figure near the windows with the light to his back.

"Oh, sure. We can leave right away." Ann pulled her handbag out of a desk drawer. She was being a coward and she knew it. But this wasn't the way she'd planned for her father to meet Joe.

From the corner of her eye, she saw the inevitable moment of encounter. Planned or not, the time had come. With a forced smile, she turned. Following her movement, her father also turned to face the approaching figure.

"Dad, this is Joe Tannerhill," she said. "Joe, this is my father, James Stapleton."

"How do you do sir." Joe smiled and extended his hand.

Her father's stare was one of shock as Joe wrapped his long, black fingers around his white hand.

"How do you do," her father replied automatically.

"Dad's taking me to lunch," Ann said.

"Fine," Joe nodded, "I think we have the Memphis papers in order. Take the rest of the day if you like."

"I intend to," Ann replied crisply to that pointed and unnecessary remark, aware of her father's increasing irritation.

"You must be very proud of your daughter, sir. She's the backbone of my campaign."

"Yes," Stapleton said without smiling.

"Let's go, Dad," Ann said, taking his arm and leading

him out the door without as much as a goodbye for Joe.

In the revolving restaurant on top of the Renaissance Center, She tried to make happy comments, describing landmarks of the city, Belle Isle, the boats on the Detroit River, the Canadian shoreline. But her father was unresponsive to her efforts.

He broke in. "Ann, is this what you want? Is this the job you wrote about?"

"Well, yes," she said defensively.

"This isn't what I envisioned for you. I thought by this time you'd be situated with some good publication. Maybe even be an assistant editor by now."

"Dad..."

"Now I know you've always had liberal tendencies, just like your mother, but I hoped you'd matured enough to see where those ideas would lead. I can't see you buried away here wasting all your fine talent for nothing."

"Dad." Ann reached for his hand across the table, "I'm not wasting my talent. I write for this campaign. I manage the whole thing. It's great experience. I'm not giving anything up and I'm not going to do this forever. It's just for -- maybe -- a little longer."

"Ann, you're not involved with him -- I mean -- personally, are you?"

"Of course not." She laughed, "It's only a job."

He sighed. "Glad to hear that because much as I'd like grandchildren, I just can't imagine bouncing one of them on my knee."

"Oh, Dad." Ann winced inwardly. "It's nothing like that, but frankly, you'll have to look to Gordon for grandchildren. I have no prospects."

"Nonsense. You'd have plenty of prospects if you'd get out in the right society. A beautiful girl like you. Now, Now," he raised his hand against her protest, "I may be your father but I'm not blind. You're a knockout and you know it."

"Well. Okay," she smiled and relaxed a little as she traced an imaginary design with her finger on the table, "Give me a year or two. Maybe I'll surprise you."

"I hope so, but no more surprises like today. Okay?"

Early the next morning they left for Memphis. Joe and Ann rode alone in his car, the silence between them intense.

The road noise filled the car with a deafening monotone.

Suddenly Joe pounded his ear lightly with the heel of his hand. "I can't stand all this chatter."

Ann turned toward him. "Why don't you find yourself a nice black girl and get married? There's nothing wrong with you is there?"

"There's nothing wrong with me. I don't see you dating anyone."

"There's a lot of things you don't see," she returned hotly, "You don't see anyone but yourself. You don't care about anyone else's feelings but your own."

"Look," he said, "I'm sorry if I caused your father any discomfort." He paused, "I don't know what to do about you." Joe glanced over at her, unsmiling, his eyes dark and accusing, "Why don't I have a wife? I think you know why. You just can't deal with it."

"Don't talk foolishness." Ann frowned and turned again to the window, her heart beating wildly.

At the hotel in Memphis, while the others were downstairs seeing to last minute details, Ann was upstairs in the room that was Joe's office during his stay. She was making last minute notes for his discussion later that evening.

Joe and Belle came in together, laughing. How charming he looked, less reserved, less austere. She envied Belle their shared heritage.

Belle smiled, waved to Ann and winked as she passed through to the adjoining room.

"What would you say, Ann, if I told you I've decided to take your advice," Joe said. "I'm thinking seriously of asking the woman I love to marry me."

"Good. That's fine. Congratulations," she answered

almost choking on the words.

He walked to her, leaned over and looked into her face.

"That's fine? Congratulations? That's it? You don't even give a damn who?"

"You want me to say it tears me up? Well it doesn't." Her words, cold and bitter, shot off her tongue as she stood and glared at him. "You should get married. It would help your campaign. I've always said so."

"My campaign? That's what's important to you?"

"Of course it is. You're my job. If you look good, I look good. I write your speeches. I created your image. I created you. Why Joe, I am you."

Joe slammed his fist on the table. "You work for me. You write for me, but you are not me. What you are is a damned machine, a busy little bee." He raked his fingers through his hair. "You know what Ann? Why don't you just go buzz around in someone else's life?"

Ann surged to her feet. "Thanks. I'll do just that." She slapped the yellow sheets on the floor at his feet and strode out, pushing blindly past Kip at the door.

A few minutes later a knock sounded softly at Ann's door.

"Who is it?"

"Kip."

"Oh. Okay. Just a minute." She let him in,

Kip saw the partly filled suitcase. "Why are you packing, Ann?"

"Why? Because I can't deal with this job anymore. That's why."

"What about tonight? Joe's counting on you."

"Joe. Joe. Everything's Joe. What about the rest of us? Does he care?"

"Come on, Ann. How plain does he have to make it?"

"He made it as plain as he needs to. He told me to buzz off."

"Ann, can't you see he loves you?"

"Oh, Kip, you don't understand anything, do you?" She

kissed him on the cheek and he blushed.

"I understand more than you think. I wish you'd reconsider and stay on."

"I …." She drew her lips in tightly, "I don't think I can."

"Well, I'll look for you tonight. Hope I see you."

"I don't know. If not, I'll say so-long now. It was good knowing you, Kip."

"Thanks. Here too."

Ann went to hear Joe's speech; she just didn't sit with him, Kit or Belle. When he addressed the audience, her written words came from his mouth, but something was missing.

Later, after the handshakes and discussions, the entire gathering moved to the lounge for dancing and cocktails.

Ann stood to leave.

"May I have this dance," a man sitting at the next asked her. With a glance in Joe's direction, she accepted.

Ann moved gracefully to the music, smiled and made the right comments. It all came naturally, this was she'd been raised to do. The man was handsome, witty, and white. Everything her father would want it. *But he's not what I want.*

When he led her back to the table, she excused herself to go to the rest room.

As Ann washed her hands, Belle came in.

She walked to Ann.

"Are you out of reach," Belle asked softly.

"What?"

"That's what Joe fears."

"He's not for me, Belle. He needs someone like you, beautiful and educated."

"And black? He loves you, you know."

Ann turned toward the rest room door. "Sometimes love isn't enough."

When Ann exited the elevator, she could see Joe standing in front of her room. She pushed by him, unlocked the door and entered, leaving the door open behind her.

"I don't have anything to drink," she said without turning around.

"That's all right. I don't want anything to drink."

"Well?" she turned to him, "What do you want?"

"To talk. Maybe to dance. I watched you. You dance beautifully. We've never danced."

Why not? At least she'd have this.

Without a word, Ann went to a wall switch and turned it. Soft music filled the room. She faced him, waited.

Joe put both arms around her in an embrace rather than the usual dance pose.

Ann's heart raced as she closed her eyes and swayed slowly to the rhythm of the music.

"Why do you hold me off," he asked.

She couldn't reply.

"You make my guts melt. Understand?" Joe's husky voice was unlike anything she had ever heard from him before.

She pressed her head against his chest.

"I want to make love to you," he said.

"I can't. We can't."

"Dear God, Ann. I love you. And you love me, too. Don't you? Why can't you say it?"

"Do you need the words?"

"Yes. I need the words. It's only you and I here. No one else. Say it. Tell me you love me.'

"Oh, Joe." Her hands slipped inside his coat, across the smooth silkiness of his shirt, the breadth of his shoulders. How many times had she dreamed of doing this? How many times had she imagined being held in his arms? She slowly moved her hands to his chest, one finger finding its way under a button of his shirt.

There was a knock at the door.

Joe grabbed her hands. "They'll go away."

"No." She stepped back from him, smoothed her dress, "I have to see who it is."

She went quickly to the door and opened it to Kip, who stepped in, took one look at Joe, and said, "Oh. I'm sorry. Am

I interrupting something?"

"No," Ann assured him, "Not at all."

"Well," Kip continued awkwardly, "I just stopped to say I was glad to see you downstairs tonight. That's all. You looked great."

"Thanks," Ann smiled, "You looked pretty good yourself."

"Is that all?" Joe said.

"Yeah." Kip shrugged. "That's all. Guess I'll go to bed now."

Ann's moment of weakness had passed. What had she been thinking? If Kip hadn't come…? She pushed the thought away. It would be best to keep Kip in the room with them. "Sorry I can't offer you something. I didn't expect company, but I can call room service."

Joe stared at her for a long moment, and then turned away. "Not for me," he said. "I'd like to stop and see my aunt on the way home. Not too far from here. Ann, would you like to meet her?"

What could she say? No, she didn't want to meet her. No, she wasn't leaving with him. Hadn't, she already quit? Why were they doing this to each other? "I'd love to meet her." She heard herself say.

Joe and Ann arrived at his aunt's house at about noon. It was a small, white frame in an old, rural part of the state.

Lily Brown was tall and thin with brittle gray hair tied in a tight knot at the back of her head.

Ann felt her cool acceptance all the way to her toes. After a few minutes of stilted conversation, she asked Joe to go to the storage shed and bring in a melon.

Lily Brown turned to Ann. "What you want with our boy?"

"We work together," Ann replied.

"You twist his head. I see it. We got good girls here want to marry him."

"With my blessing." Ann looked at Joe's aunt, the only family he had left. She understood her wanting to keep Joe with his own people. "Believe me," she continued, "I have no intentions of twisting his head."

Joe returned with the melons. "Look at these beauties. They're just right to eat."

"Here, Honey, let me fix 'em," His aunt took the melons, and as she cut them added, "Why don't you go see Ida Mae while you're here? She been askin' 'bout you. She's right pretty, too. All growed up. Gone to college and real smart. Jes like you, Honey."

Joe glanced at Ann and smiled.

"I'm sure she is, Aunt Lil'," he said, "but we won't have time for that."

"Why not?" Ann said. "I could spend some time in town, stay at a hotel there tonight, and we could start back tomorrow."

Joe's eyes hardened. "No. It would mean an additional day away from work. We have to head back this afternoon. The election's in less than three weeks and we still have a lot to do."

They left Aunt Lily's at three o'clock and headed home. Ann was determined to keep the atmosphere light and to ignore the personal antagonism beneath the surface.

They sped along the two lane country road with the windows down, breathing in the sweet southern air.

Toward early evening Joe pulled up at a roadside café and entered a small dining room. Two men wearing overalls leaned against the counter conversing with the cook while a third played the pinball machine. All looked to be in their late twenties or early thirties. Ann and Joe walked to a small table and sat down.

The one in the cook's apron called over, not bothering to come to them. "You want sumpin?"

"Yes. We'll have coffee to start," Joe said and picked up a menu.

The two men at the counter puckered their lips as though to whistle and turned to the cook for his response. After a brief, silent deliberation, the cook poured one cup of coffee from a pot on the back burner, brought it around the end of the counter and, when he reached the table, spilled the contents in Joe's lap.

"Why you clumsy ass," Joe snapped, jumping up.

"Oh, say, was that hot, boy?" the cook inquired with mock dismay.

The two men at the counter moved to the table and stood beside the cook. The pinball machine became silent.

"That was a little accident," the cook said, "and for your information, we don't serve niggers in here and we sure as hell don't abide niggers cohortin' with white women no how. Git it, boy?"

Joe drew back his arm with fist ready, "Why you … "

"Hey. Hold it. Hold it," Ann shouted, springing up between them as the three men closed ranks around the cook. "We're not cohorting. He works for me. We're just passing through."

With a glare at Ann, Joe turned and stomped out of the restaurant.

"Yeah?" The cook was unconvinced.

"Yes. We just stopped in for an early dinner. I told him to come in. That's all."

"Miss, we don't believe in mixin' the races."

"Well, neither do we," Ann said as she moved to follow Joe.

At the door, one of the men waited.

"Ya know, it's gitten' kinda late, Miss," he said, "Aincha kinds 'fraid o' bein' alone with that nigger in that thare car?"

"Not at all," she said with mimicked indolence, and then added, "Daddy had him castrated."

"I'll be damned," he smiled.

"Quite possibly," she responded as she walked out the door, knowing her quip was lost on him.

In the car, Joe sat fuming.

"Get over here and open this door for me," she said between her teeth.

"The hell I will," he growled, staring straight ahead, hands gripping the steering wheel.

She opened the door herself, knowing the men in the café were watching the black man's defiance, and climbed into the back seat.

She was hardly in when Joe gunned the motor and ripped away, causing her to fall heavily against the seat.

"I work for you?" he snapped, "I work for you? You're just like them. Keeping up the old stereotypes. I should have left you there. You'd fit right in."

"Where would you be now if you'd hit him? Dead probably, or in jail. And then what? If you lived and got out, that scandal would follow you throughout your career. You'd never be able to live it down. *'Joseph Tannerhill, a candidate for the United States Congress, jailed following fist fight in Tennessee.'*"

He didn't reply, but she heard his heavy breathing.

"So you just sit there, nurse your black pride and keep on driving. I just hope we get out of here with our skins all in one peace."

As darkness fell, Ann's mood relaxed. It seemed certain they would reach the interstate safely."Are you okay," she asked.

"Yeah, but I'd be a lot better if you'd come up and sit beside me."

"We're not in the clear yet," she cautioned.

"Who's gonna see in the dark? You can climb over the seat. I won't even have to stop."

After a moment's hesitation, over the seat she went. When she was settled, they smiled at each other and Joe took hold of her hand.

"When we're in the clear I'm going to pull over. There's something I want to say." He glanced at her with a determined expression. Ann turned to the window. She didn't want to hear what he would say, especially when she wasn't sure she could resist him any longer.

Joe glanced in the rear view mirror and Ann detected a

change in him.

"What's the matter?"

"There's a car coming up on us --fast."

She stiffened and looked behind them. In a moment the car was close enough to pass. As it came along side of them, it drew in close and brushed their car.

"Why don't they just pass?" Ann cried.

"Hold on," Joe said. "It's that jerk cook and you can bet he's not alone." He pressed the accelerator hard and they shot ahead.

The car followed, bumping, pushing, while Joe tried to keep their car in front.

"Where in hell's that interstate?" he said.

The car struck again, Joe swerved and the right front tire went off the road. He gunned the engine, but they must have landed in mud, because the tires just spun in place.

"Is your door locked?" Ann cried.

Before Joe could reach the button, the door was torn open and the grinning face of the cook peered in at them."

"Well now, boy, we's jes gonna see if you're castrated like she says. 'Cause if you ain't, you will be."

They grabbed Joe and began to pull him out of the car.

"Let him go. Let him go," Ann screamed.

They dragged Joe into the road.

One of the men jerked Ann from the car. With a feral snarl, she raked her nails down the side of his face.

"Why you damn little nigger-lovin' bitch," the man screamed, "I'll knock them teeth out o' yer mouth 'fore I'm done with you," and he let loose with a blow intended for her mouth but it landed on her cheek as she turned her head just in time;.

Over his shoulder Ann saw car lights approaching.

"Take that nigger in the swamp." The man holding her ordered.

"Thare's snakes in thare," one objected.

"Well, it's maybe snakes or a for sure eyewitness out here."

Flashing red lights appeared atop the fast approaching

car.

"It's the damn sheriff." One of the men grumbled.

The sheriff stopped his car beside them, headlights at high beam.

The searchlight moved over the group.

"Let that girl go," the sheriff ordered as he got out of his car and approached them. "The man too."

The men released their captives.

"Now you boys git on out o' here afore I run y'all in," the sheriff said.

"We weren't gonna kill 'em." One man offered.

"Shut up an' git out o' here," the sheriff snapped.

The men turned toward their car.

The sheriff looked at Joe's car. "Wait a minute," he said to the men "Git that car out o' the mud first."

"Hell no," one said, "We ain't pushin' no nigger's car."

The sheriff pulled out his gun. "Git it out o' thare, or I'm callin' for assistance and takin' all a ya in."

The men stood, glared, one took a step toward their car and the sheriff fired a shot in the dirt at his feet.

The men scrambled to Joe's car, pushed and dug until it was free and back on the road.

"I want the names of those men, Sheriff," Joe said, "If you think they're going to get away with this threat to me and Miss Stapleton, you're mistaken."

"Now, just a minute thare, boy," the sheriff began.

My name is not 'Boy'," Joe corrected, "It's Mister Tannerhill. And I intend to bring charges… "

"Well, now, Mister Tannerhill," the sheriff interrupted. "How you gonna bring charges? I mean, what charge would you bring? They didn't do nothin' to you. You best better let it drop."

"They wrecked my car for one thing. With or without your cooperation, I can find out who they are and I'll subpoena you to testify."

The sheriff scratched his head. "Well, now, I can't testify on sumpin' I never saw." He squinted at Joe. "You best better leave it be, Mister Tannerhill. Now, why don't you and the young lady git in your car and git on your way. I'll escort you to the interstate. It's almost three miles up ahead. You won't be havin' no more trouble."

"Come on, Joe," Ann said, her teeth chattering, "I'll drive."

Under smoldering protest, Joe got in on the driver's side and slid over. Ann got behind the wheel and as they drove away, the sheriff followed. Joe sat in stoic silence. When they reached the interstate the sheriff blinked his lights as a signal of departure and Ann tooted her horn a couple of times and waved her hand as she pulled on to the northbound on-ramp.

After a new mile of tenseness, Joe finally broke the silence. "You told them I was castrated? You told them that? You said such a thing?"

"I only wanted to calm them down."

"What did you think they do after an idea like that was put into their thick Klan heads? You're just like them."

It was the second time Joe had said that and her own anger flared. "I'm not like them. I'm not a bigot about your color or mine, but you are."

"I've a right to be."

"No, no you don't."

They exchanged no further words.

It was midnight before Ann saw a Holiday Inn sign and pulled off the interstate. She drove up in front with an abrupt stop that made Joe almost bounce against the dashboard. She jerked the keys from the ignition, got out, unlocked the trunk, grabbed her suitcase, slammed the lid shut, walked around the passenger's side and threw the keys at Joe through the open window.

"We were crazy to even begin this. I'm getting out of your life, and you stay out of mine." Ann turned and walked away. Part of her screamed for him to stop her; tell her they could make it work. Joe didn't and she kept walking.

Two hours later Ann opened her motel room door. She walked out, suitcase in hand, closed the door quietly behind her. She walked to the check in counter, handed a sealed envelope and a ten dollar bill to the clerk. "Please make sure Mister Tannerhill in room two-fourteen gets this."

"Of course. Would you like me to call you a cab?"

Ann smiled. "I already have."

She walked two blocks to an all night coffee shop she had seen as they arrived. Her taxi arrived ten minutes later. As they passed the motel, she blinked back tears. "It's for the best Joe. For both of us."

Ann knew the note would hurt him. He'd want to come after her. She hoped her simple words would stop him. She had written.

Dear Joe,

Here are the words you want to hear…yes I love you, but sometimes love isn't enough. The past two days have made that clear. I'm going home. If you really love me, then let me go. Please don't contact me, Joe. It will only make things harder.

Ann

One Month Later

Ann was no longer at war with herself or with Joe. Some things just weren't meant to be, and needless to say, her father was overjoyed she was no longer with the black candidate from Michigan. Even after the election, her father refused to acknowledge Joe's victory. When she'd said, "We won the election." Her father was shocked and angered.

"What do you mean we?" He'd said, regarding her with annoyance.

"Well, we all worked for it, Belle, Kip and I. We all contributed. So we all won."

"His success," her father had stressed. "You aren't affiliated with him, so it's his success."

Ann had shrugged. Joe was out of her life, so there was no sense arguing and she'd let the subject drop.

In her bedroom, Ann walked to the chair in front of the

window and settled into it. It was almost two and she hadn't eaten since this morning, but food didn't sound good to her. She knew she'd lost weight in the past month, pounds she could ill afford to drop. A knock sounded on her bedroom door. "Yes."

"Ann, it's your mother. May I come in?"

"Sure, Mom."

Candace Stapleton walked into the room and straight to Ann's side. "I've let this go on long enough. It's time to stop."

"What, Mom?"

"You're not eating. You mope around the house, or you sit here and stare out the window."

"It's only been a month," Ann said defensively. "I haven't decided what I want to do yet."

"Oh, Ann, you do know what you want to do. Why haven't you done it?"

Ann blinked back tears. "I told him not to follow me, and he didn't. How can..."

"Do you love him?"

Ann stood walked to the calendar. Today was Valentines's Day. The day of love. Maybe, but not for her.

"Ann, you didn't answer me. Do you love Joe?"

"Love isn't enough, Mom. It doesn't make people colorblind. Joe's a congressman now. He's forgotten about me."

"Ann..."

"I don't want to talk about it anymore. I'm going for a walk."

Ann saw the back of the taxi as she turned into the driveway.

Robbins, their houseman, opened the door for her.

"You just missed the fireworks, Miss Stapleton," he said.

"What do you mean?"

"Congressman Tannerhill was here. That was him leaving in that taxi."

"Joe was here?"

"He came to talk to your father."

"Dear God. I'm sure that went well."

Robbins smiled. "I heard the shouting even from out here. The congressman wanted to see you. Mister Stapleton said you weren't here, that you'd never be here for the likes of him."

"Father said that?"

"Yes, and much more."

She touched his arm. "I'm sorry you had to hear that, Robbins. Daddy can be...."

"I understand, Miss Stapleton. I've worked here for thirty years." Robbins grinned. "Your father kicked the congressman out. Said he wasn't welcome here, and that he'd better stay away from you. But Mister Tannerhill stood right up to him, hollered as loud as your daddy, said it was up to you, not him, if he was to see you again."

Joe had come for her. A giant weight lifted off her heart. Ann moved by Robbins. "Thank you. I'll take it from here.

"Your father's in his study."

Her father stood in front of the fireplace staring into the flames. "Dad?"

He turned. "Ann, I have a great idea. How would you would like to take a European vacation? Maybe the south of France for the winter, or maybe Greece. What do you think? Could you be ready in a day or two?"

"Dad, I know Joe was here."

Her father scowled. "You will not see him, Ann. I forbid it."

"I'm not a child, Dad. I'm a grown woman."

"Promise me, Ann. Promise you won't see him."

"Dad, I can't promise that."

"Why? Why do you have to see him?"

"I love you, Dad, and as much as I know how it will hurt you to hear it, I'm in love with Joe."

"Forget him, Ann. He's black. You told me once you weren't involved with Tannerhill. Was that a lie?"

"I wasn't. I'm still not. But I realize I didn't allow

myself to be involved with him because of you. I tried to live my life to please you, but not anymore. I love him. Please try to understand."

Her father turned away.

With a sigh Ann walked from the room. In the entry way she turned to Robbins. "Did Congressman Tannerhill say where he was staying?"

"At the Royce Inn," her mother said from the upstairs balcony. "I heard him tell your father."

"Thanks Mom. I love you."

Ann turned toward Robbins, who held her coat and scarf. With a trembling hand she took both and ran out the door.

At the Royce Inn, Ann pushed through the revolving glass doors and directly into Joe.

"Ann, at last," he said as he folded her in his arms.

"Oh, Joe," she said, ignoring the stares of people around them as she raised her eyes to his, "I love you."

"I know. Ann, will you marry me?"

"Just as soon as you ask me."

"I'm asking. Will you?"

"Yes. Yes. Yes."

## Author's Bio: Thelma Flory Walker

After her father's death in 1970, Thelma began collecting information from her mother about her maternal grandmother's life so that she could write her fictionalized story. That book. *Footsteps of Yesterday,* was published in 2003. She is now working on a sequel.

She has written many short stories and presently has poems published in two international literary works. *A Proud Little Pot* appears in Timeless Voices, a volume of poems by The International Library of Poetry, and *Sister* appears in Centres of Expression, a Noble House publication.

Retiring from the Office of Criminal Justice Planning in 1980, she lives in Santa Maria, California with her dog and two cats. She has been a member of the writers group, Word Wizards, since 2000.

# Love's Pathway

by: Cathleen Thompson

Today starts our life together,
Engraving dazzling memories
In this frazzled world.

Love deep within each other's hearts'
Grow prisms of crystal sparkle,
Reflect and protect each day.

Lifetime glows bright
With insight in years to come.
Twist and turn down pathway,
With many lessons learned.

Relationship grows
Being apart or near,
In face of fear.

Flames of love,
Grow strong and true.

A tapestry of deeply colored textures,
Enrich our life stitch by stitch,
Etching patterns of love everlasting.

## Party Time

by: Sylva Mularchyk

Balancing two awkward packages on one arm and a sack of groceries on the other, I staggered up the walk to my house, backed into the door, pushed it open, and practically fell into the kitchen. I put the grocery bag on the counter, the packages on the table, and rubbed my tired arms. But there was no time to waste—I had a birthday cake to bake and party decorations to prepare and all before six-o-clock. I'd promised Joey he could invite three friends this year.

I glanced out the window to see if Joey was coming. He always watched the street from Mrs. Murphy's house and sometimes arrived home almost before I did. Mrs. Murphy was jolly and kind. Too kind, maybe. She often spoiled his dinner with her home baked cookies. Since today was both Valentine's Day and Joey's birthday I was sure she'd went overboard.

My thoughts ran on. It's my own fault Joey doesn't have a stay-at-home mom. He could have a real, live step-father and I wouldn't have to work... if I could make up my mind. *Dear David, you have been gone more than three years; and although I miss you more than I can say, I have to consider Joey's fatherless life.*

Until I'd met Bryce Gordon at the office picnic, I had toyed with the idea of accepting Phil Potter's proposal of marriage. Then, as if the choice between Bryce and Phil had not been difficult enough, a new teacher came to Woodville. Tall and robust, he was really quite handsome in spite of the thick-lens glasses. Only six weeks after we'd met, Larry Courtland proposed to me. Ever since, I'd had a frantic time keeping my datebook in order, trying to keep the three men from crossing paths.

I just couldn't decide. Each would be a fine husband in his own way. I loved going dancing with Phil. An evening at a play or a concert with Bryce was equally fun and maybe a bit more satisfying in an intellectual way. Swimming or hiking with Larry was great any time. But it wasn't only their social assets that attracted me to each of them. They were all successful men in their fields. Larry Courtland happened to be Joey's teacher and Cub Scout Leader. Bryce was the assistant editor of our local newspaper.

But back to basics. I put the cake in the oven just as my son came through the door. "Oh, Joey, do you know what I forgot? The candles for the cake. Can you run up to the store and get some?"

"Sure, Mom. Oh, I called my friends this morning—they all said they could come to my party."

"Fine, Joey. You didn't call more than three, did you? I don't feel I can handle more than that this year."

"Just three, Mom. And I used my beat manners, too—just according to Emily Post." Joey had an 'according to' for everything. "Don't worry, Mom. They'll be good. They promised." He started out the door.

I sighed gratefully. I do hope they behave themselves. Last year, Butch tore the sash off Susan's dress and..." I decided not to go on.

The telephone rang in the living room and I dashed to answer it. "Hello."

"Hello, Marla. You sound as if you've been running."

I recognized Joey's teacher's voice. "Yes, I have, Larry. Today is a busy day. It's Joey's birthday."

"I know. That's why I'm calling. Joey invited me to his party. I'm calling to see what he might like for a present."

I gasped. "Joey invited you? But Larry, you can't be serious. This is a children's party."

"So it's a children's party." Larry said, unperturbed. "I realize I'm Joey's teacher and all, but that doesn't preclude him from inviting me to his party, or does it?"

"I suppose not. But I just thought you might feel a little out of place among the other children—I mean the other guests."

He chuckled. "Well, that's settled, Marla. Let's get back to the question at hand. What do you think Joey would like as a present?"

"Just anything you would like for yourself—if you were going to be eleven."

"Fair enough." Larry chuckled. "I don't blame you for being upset, Marla, but this was Joey's idea. After all, I couldn't hurt his feelings and refuse to come to his party, could I?"

"I'm not upset. If Joey wants you to come, then so do I." I wondered what my son had in mind. Could it be that he was trying to play Cupid? It would be a most unusual party—one adult, three children.

Joey came back with the candles, and I told him that one of his guests had called.

"You said I could ask whoever I wanted—"

"I know. It's fine. Do you really like Mr. Courtland that well?"

"Gosh, Mom, he's swell."

The phone rang again as Joey shut the bathroom door.

"Hello, Marla, honey."

It was Phil Potter. Big, jovial Phil.

"I won't keep you long. I just called to see if you could give me a hint as to what Joey would like for his birthday."

"You don't have to get him anything, Phil."

"It wouldn't look right if I didn't bring him a present after he invited me to his party. I was thinking of a football. How does that sound?"

"Yes, I believe he would l like that very much. Phil, do you know that Larry Courtland is coming, too?"

"He is? Well, I suppose he already knows how to play pin-the-tail-on-the-donkey. We should get along very well together—if we're blindfolded."

I put the phone down and stared at it. The party was becoming more and more strange. Two adults and two children. Then the doorbell rang and I had a funny feeling as to who it might be. Even though a sixth sense told me who it was, I was still flustered when I opened the door to Bryce Gordon.

"Hello, Marla. I called you a short time ago, but your phone was busy. Joey invited me to his birthday party, and I don't know what to give him. Do you think he'd like a set of toy soldiers?"

Even though I'd guessed who Joey's third guest would be, I was still a bit unhinged.

When I didn't answer, Bryce continued. "Perhaps that isn't such a good idea for a boy as intelligent as Joey. After all, I was thinking of a chess set, too. Marla, are you all right?"

"Of course, I am. But Bryce, I think it's only fair to tell you there will be two other guests."

"I know. I think Joey said he'd asked three friends in all."

"And he did. He asked you, and Phil Potter and Larry Courtland. Three friends."

There was a tiny twitch at the corner of his lip—almost a smile. "A most interesting selection. Joey has more finesse than I realized. I am going to get him the chess set after all. Well, see you later."

"Until later," I murmured.

Whatever will they talk about? Larry and his youth activities. Phil and his amusing anecdotes. Bryce and his books and music. Why, they haven't a thing in common. What was Joey thinking?

Sometime after six that evening, cheerful voices in the living room spilled into the kitchen where I arranged eleven candles on a peppermint-striped cake. The voices broke into song as I entered.

"For he's a jolly good fellow..."

Joey's happy laughter warmed me. I leaned down to him, and saw the reflected glow of the candles flicker in his eyes.

"Now for the wish," Phil said. "You must always make a birthday wish before you blow out the candles!"

Joey squeezed his eyes shut as if to think. Then he drew his breath, leaned forward and with one great *whoosh* blew out all the candles.

"Great, Joey. Now you will get your wish!

"What was it?" Phil asked.

"But he mustn't tell, " I broke in quickly, "or it won't come true." Who knew what strange wish Joey might have made?

I thought about how careful I had been with Phil, Bryce and Larry. How adroitly I had managed to date first one and then the other and then the other without their paths ever crossing. With one bold stroke, Joey had brought the three of them together. How amicable they were.

They had come to Joey's party and Joey's guests they had remained. They deferred to me only as Joey's mother. They had bandied a dozen subjects about, always with Joey as the center of attention. The oddest part was that they all seemed to be having a wonderful time.

I stood apart after they had finished their cake and ice cream and the business of opening the gifts began. According to our family tradition, Joey put my package aside for last.

He was excited over the football from Phil. "I'll teach you some passes I used to make," Phil promised.

Joey untied the ribbons around Larry's small package and exclaimed. "Woowee! A Cub Scout knife. Look, Mom. Is it ever keen!"

"Now you can show the rest of the Cubs a thing or two about camping." Larry said and grinned.

Joey placed the shiny knife beside the football and reached for the square box that was Bryce's present. "A chess set," he said softly as he folded back the wrapping paper. He lifted out the king piece and turned to Bryce. "Will you teach me how to castle?"

"Sure, I will. Castling isn't as difficult as it sounds."

"Why, Joey, I didn't know you knew how to play chess," I said in surprise."

"I don't, really, Mom. But there was a book at school that showed pictures of all the pieces and how to make some opening plays. I wanted to learn, but I wanted to learn right. You know, according to Hoyle or something."

How little I knew my son! I had never dreamed such a thing as chess would appeal to him. Already he was entering a world of his own about which I knew nothing.

"Mom, you've got to sit beside me while I open your present." It was a relief to sit down on the sofa. The wrappings came away quickly. "Gosh, Mom, how did you know I wanted a bow and arrow? It's super."

I accepted his warm, sticky kiss and my heart thumped so happily it hurt. "But you remember what I told you about following the safety regulations and—"

"Of course, Mom. You only mentioned that every time I told you I would like a real bow and arrow—and I promise to follow all the rules of safety according to—"

"Yes, Joey. I know you will."

There was a little clapping by the men—then suddenly, the party was over and Larry was saying, "Can we help with the cleanup, Marla?"

"Of course not, Larry. Guests never do the dishes."

"I sure thank you all for coming," Joey was saying. "And thanks again for the great presents, too. It was the nicest party ever and that's according to me!"

The three men hesitated at the door, and suddenly they seemed like three little boys who know the party was over, but weren't yet ready to leave. Oddly, Joey who had been so articulate all evening seemed to be having difficulties in bidding his guests good night. There was an air of unfinished business in the way the men stood there, each waiting for the others to leave first.

They can't all stay, I thought firmly, wondering how I could break the news that I had made up my mind, for now I knew which man I wanted to marry. It wasn't dear Larry—so wholesome, so full of never-ending energy. He could be a pal for Joey, but there was more to life than one long camping trip. And Phil? I had known him the longest. He would always provide a good home, and we'd know a lot of fun people. But somehow, it wasn't enough.

What did Bryce have to offer that was so special? It was a quality too elusive for me to name. I had felt it for the first time this evening. Was it the chess set that had shown me the man I needed—the man I wanted—the man who had seen in my son the wish and the ability to think and plan ahead? That man knew how to stimulate the best part of Joey—and by doing so, he somehow enhanced my own feeling of worth.

The men were already crossing the lawn on the way to their cars, when I looked down at my son. "Joey, will you call Bryce back? Tell him I have something very important to say to him."

Joey's eyes sparkled. "Mom, do you know what? You just made my Valentine's Day wish come true, too!"

He waited only long enough to catch the kiss I threw before he ran down the porch steps. "Hey, Bryce. Mom would like to see you!"

## Author's Bio: Sylva Mularchyk

Sylva Mularchyk was born in Washington, D. C., where her father, a soldier, was stationed. Her father's first civilian job was as the Agency Farmer on the Blackfeet Indian Reservation at Heart Butte, Montana. Her mother taught the school which Sylva attended. The family moved to North Dakota and again to Montana. When Sylva married, they moved to Bremerton, Washington. Here she worked in the Puget Sound Naval Shipyard. Later, when she divorced, she transferred to a civilian position for the U.S. Air Force and went to Spain where she began seriously to write and take photographs. She spent many years in Europe. Her articles and short stories were translated into other languages. When she retired and returned to America, she settled in California. Sylva has three children: daughter Beverley in Alaska; Bill, a postal supervisor in Seattle, WA and Ted, in the retail industry in California.

## And the Reason My Book Never Got Published Is….

by: Ann Schafer

"It's too long."

"It's too short."

"Too dull. The characters are flat."

"There's too much action. Too many people doing too many things. Confusing. And the plot stinks."

Yeah, yeah, yeah—if you ever wrote a book, or know anybody who did, and the manuscript got sent out to publishers, I bet some of those excuses for it never getting accepted and published showed up in the mailbox. But I have another one, one I'm sure you never heard of before and probably never will again.

You see, it all started one night when I was sitting in the bar just yakking with Louie the bartender about nothin' in particular when some guy sitting on the stool next to me—who thought he knew it all—butted in and started telling us how he works for this high-class publishing company, and they're always on the lookout for new authors.

"Oh, yeah," Louie smirked. "I bet I've heard enough stories here to write a dozen books."

"Well," our new friend replies, "it has to be something fresh, something with innovative ideas, to even get looked at." Then he adds that there's supposed to be only eight or nine different story lines in the whole world. And if anybody could come up with a tenth one, he would be rich and famous. Now me and Louie wouldn't know an innovative idea if it walked up and said, "Good morning."

Louie just laughed. "Guess that's the end of my writing career."

For some reason that I never did figure out, the stranger's words stuck with me. I couldn't get them out of my head. Sometimes I woke up at night thinking about it. Then, one day I knew, I just knew, I had that tenth story.

Right here, you got to realize a couple of things. First, I'm not the kind of guy who hangs around the library looking up references and checking out books. Second, this was a few years back before computers and a bunch of these other gadgets became so popular. Not that I'm the kind of guy you'd normally find using them, either.

Anyway, I got this one terrific idea for a great story, so I bought a bunch of big yellow pads and sharpened up some pencils. And I started to write. I even went to the library to work on it 'cause I knew none of my pals would see me there, and I didn't want to have to do no explaining just in case one of 'em dropped by my place unexpected like. Besides, that seemed more author-like than just sittin' at the kitchen table.

After I come up with this wonderful opening sentence—*It was a dark and stormy night*—that story just seemed to tell itself. Hell, I was using words I didn't even know I knew. Well, to keep this particular story short, I'll tell you it took me just about a year to get it all down. When I was done, I knew for positive I had one great book anyone would give his right arm to publish. I mean who wouldn't jump at a chance to read a book starting out like mine did?

Since I lived in New York at the time, I just looked up one of the publishing companies in the 'Yellow Pages' and went down to the office. I had gathered all the pages of my manuscript together and numbered them to make it easy to read. Then I stuffed them in this old shirt box and tied it good and tight with some heavy string. I mean, can you imagine what I'd of had to do if it fell apart on the subway or somethin'?

When I finally found the place, it was halfway up to the top of a skyscraper, a real first-rate-lookin' establishment. The girl at the front desk looked real high class with her silvery blond hair swept back from her face and an outfit that didn't start you thinking of monkey business—the kind of person you'd want people to think of when your company was mentioned. But would you believe it—that girl at the desk didn't want to touch my manuscript. Why, I even had to untie the box myself. When she saw the stack of yellow paper, she said, in a voice that would have froze a polar bear, "The editors really preferred it be typed."

I asked her was she willing to do it, and she didn't seem to think that was even a little bit funny. And I mean it wasn't like I was expecting her to do it for free or nothin'. I offered to take her to lunch at the deli I'd seen a couple blocks away. She just stared at me with her frosty blue eyes and said something like that being against company policy.

Well, I don't need a kick in the head to know when it's time to leave, so I tied up my box and informed her there was no hard feelings just because she couldn't recognize a terrific book when it was starin' her right in the face. And I would be pleased to present her with an autographed copy when it got on the best seller list. Then I went to a phone booth and found the address of another company.

I know you won't hardly believe this, but I got the same treatment at the next place. Except here, the eyes were a chilly brown, the hair was black, and the clothes were different, but they put across the same impression. This girl said the manuscript had to be typed and in the proper format before they would look at it. Proper format—I didn't know what she was talking about, but I sure as hell wasn't going to ask.

After this happened a few more times, I come to realize that writin' a great book ain't really the hard part. The really hard part is finding some editor who's got brains enough to read it. I was pretty dejected about all this and about ready to give up the whole thing when, right after Thanksgiving, I run into an old pal, Harry Flannigan. We decided to knock back a couple drinks and headed for a nearby waterin' hole. The bar was kind of dark and smoky, but it was pretty early in the evening, so it wasn't too loud, and we found us a table towards the back. After a few rounds, I felt like he'd understand what I'd been going through, so I acquainted him with my problem.

Harry listened to the whole story, and then he said, real excited like, "Boy, I'm glad you told me. I can help you with this. My second cousin's an agent, and he works with authors all the time. He's got an office and a part-time secretary and everything. I never been there, but I'd bet it's real swanky."

"Oh, yeah," I said, "that's great, but how many publishers does he know? Does he work with them? I need a guy who can get my book into a publishing company 'cause it sure seems like I can't."

Harry reached across the table and gripped my arm. "Listen, my friend. Meet with the guy. I'm telling you, he's the one you need."

Well, what could it hurt? For certain, it couldn't hurt any worse than the hammerin' Harry was giving my hammerin' headache. That's for sure. Harry said he'd ask his cousin to come down to the bar and talk to me. So, we met, Harry's second cousin and me. He was a sharp-looking guy with slick-backed, dark hair and a skinny mustache under his nose. A diamond flashed on his pinky finger, and I swear his nails were manicured. Right away, I agreed to sign the paper he had with him. A contract was what he called it. He took my manuscript and said, as a special favor, because I was such a good friend of Harry's, he would get his secretary to type it up for me. I didn't want to seem cheap, so I give him twenty bucks for his secretary because he said it would require extra time for her. Then he said not to expect to hear from him for a month or so. Even a cool operator like him had to have some maneuvering time.

One month passed, and then two. By the time the third month was near over, I was starting to sweat. I mean that guy had the only copy of my book. I called the number on my copy of the contract—no answer. So, I looked for Harry. I figured finding him would not be too hard if I could only calculate which bar was his favorite at the moment. When I finally run him down at Jackson's, I inquired where was this great cousin of his hidin' out.

"Geeze, didn't you hear? I can't believe you haven't heard." Harry shook his head in disbelief.

"So, okay, Harry. What the hell are you talking about?" I guess I was gettin' a little loud, 'cause Harry hurried to explain.

"A couple of weeks ago—yeah, right on February fourteenth, Valentine's day, of all days—Joe found his girl, his secretary—was cheatin' on him with some guy from a publishing company. He couldn't take it, so he just up and walked out the window of his apartment. It was five stories up, and that was that. Geeze, I'd a thought somebody would've told his clients."

Well, nobody had told me, and nobody could find my manuscript either. So, one of the greatest books ever written, the one with that tenth story line, it never got published. But I bet this is the first time you ever heard of a book not getting published because a guy just walked out on you—so to speak.

## One Look

by:  Cathleen Thompson

Twinkling blue eyes
Frame handsome face
One look was all it took
Powerful energy flew
Across a crowded room

Clinking glasses
Loud background noise
The look, the eyes, the voice
Always came back to him

In a blink I realize
Good character, reliable, kind
Attraction fills the bill
Goes into overdrive

Who would believe one look
Was all it took
Find love that could thrive
Across a crowded room

## The Gift

by:  Daniel E. Wilcox

"Hey you, white boy.  Get up off that couch and get this junk outta my livin' room.  Stop feelin' sorry for yourself.  Eva's dumpin' you is no reason for you to mope.  I'm talking to you!"  Hilda yanked my leather coat with its long Cody fringe, and me, up from where I had had my head buried in its soft folds.

Even though Eva's copper-hued face still filled my consciousness, I twisted over and looked up at 'Mother' Hilda as she stared down at me, without wrinkle, just like her husband's—ageless.  I had boarded with this family the previous summer while doing volunteer work on the Cheyenne Reservation.  Now I was back on the Rez.  It was located in the sandstone foothills and low mountains of southern Montana, only a war dance away from the Little Big Horn Battlefield.

"Ja! I never seen such lazy bones!  Val, you get yerself outa here into the boys' room—you'll sleep in the twin's bed."

"Then where'll they sleep?  That's okay, I'll sleep on the floor in my bag."

"Doncha give me no back talk," she said with mock seriousness.  "It's their bed for you.  They'll sleep with us."  She swatted me with her dish towel.  "I gotta get David's supper goin'."  Her heavy form shifted around and lumbered back toward the kitchen, her rough black hair moving back and forth across the back of her faded blue print dress.

I sat up on the sagging couch—the third-time-removed, dirt-brown couch—removed from their parent's log cabin, from their own tarpaper two-room shack, finally to this, a carpeted pink-red living room in a new frame house, part of the housing project in Cheyenne Agency.  David BigShoulder was a hard worker, slowly building a better life for his family, putting in long, arduous hours as a construction worker for the BIA administration.

At dawn, Hilda had come to the door in response to my knock, seen me standing on the snowy porch, shivering with cold and full of youthful sorrow. She hugged me to her elephant form, while yelling to David, "Come out here. Our paleface has come back, and would you look at his Cody-fringed leather coat!"

I was still so tired and numb. I had lost two nights' sleep hitching northward through Nevada and Utah—contending with a blowing snowstorm and often huddled by the side of the Interstate, wrapped in my sleeping bag like some cigar store Indian—thumbing for rides. I was living in Huntington Beach in sunny California when I received Eva's 'Dear Lone Ranger' letter shortly after the new year. While I was studying the Romantic poets at Cal State Long Beach, the love of my life decided to drop me for a Cheyenne guy at her BIA high school in Lame Deer. So much for our Indian summer. Now it was February, below zero, and yet here I was back in Montana trying to make a last stand for my sweetheart.

With an effort I stood, swung my rucksack over my angular frame and clumped down the dimly-lit hall to the boys' room, then fell into deep slumber and images of Eva... her plump figure, cinnamon-colored arms extended, bending to scoop up a silver pitcher of icy water from the barrel behind her uncle's cabin. Her in a purple blouse and faded jeans standing below the tall sandstone pinnacles, looking toward me while I snapped her picture with my Kodak. Her in my arms under the silhouetted silver water tower, the stars shimmering sequin-like, the taste of berries on her tongue, from earlier when we had eaten a bowl full at her uncle's.

I woke hours later and followed the greasy aroma of fried bread and boiling deer jerky into the kitchen. Was Eva right now helping her aunt cook? "Hilda, do you think Eva might be home by now? Maybe I could call her uncle and aunt, and they could relay my message."

"Stop moonin' around about that bad letter she sent you. That girl's got no sense, nor you! Here, take this," she said, handing me a stub broom. "You sweep the floor. When David gets home, you can help him chop more wood. Here, you a smart boy and don't stay in college but run around the countryside—Ja!" She shook her head and pursed her lips. "Makes no sense..."

I started to offer a defense but retreated before her volley of mixed Cheyenne and White. Instead I pulled out the chrome chairs and swept crumbs and dust from under the table toward me, wincing in an enjoyable way as her tirade continued.

"Why'd you come up here now for jus' cause Eva's sent you that quittin' letter? What about yer learnin'? Hitchhikin' in the snow! Why I remember you when you first came into the Cheyenne Agency last June, all tall an' so pale from too much readin' in them big college rooms. You'd think you'd be all brown livin' down there in California, like in the movies. And we wondered what is this white boy doin' here. You said you ain't no BIA teacher, but was a mission assistant over to Saint Joseph's Orphanage in Ashland."

I paused the sweep of the broom. "It was a great summer—finally getting to work with Indians, falling in love with Eva... I'd been dreaming about living on the reservation since I was in Boy Scouts and earned my Indian craft merit badge."

Hilda raised her coppery-colored hands and clapped them high in the air. "Val, you ain't no boy scout. You're a darn girl scout." And she laughed, her whole large body shaking, at her own joke.

I smiled, too. "Actually, I wasn't thinking about girls at all when I arrived last summer, but of how to help at Saint Joseph's. Ever since I was about six years old, I've wanted to help the Cheyenne. My family used to get those Catholic mission appeals from the Joseph Fathers every fall. Each year they'd send out a small cardboard box with a plastic Indian. The figure had his arms extended requesting that caring Catholics send a few dollars to help in the spiritual and social development of Indians caught in poverty and sin. They'd quote from saints like Saint Valentine, reminding us to love those in need. I collected the figures along with baseball cards and model cars."

I leaned the short broom against a chair. "Then one of the fathers drove me over here to teach Vacation Bible School—teaching the story of Ruth in the Old Testament—and I met Eva; she showed up, brought her two little brothers to class. She was standing there starting to tell me their names, but I became lost in her smile, dark eyes, and soft voice that flowed over me."

"Get back to that sweepin', cause then I'm goin' have you start choppin' some of the wood. It'll surprise David. And you don't worry, Val, we'll help you an' Eva to at least get a chance to talk. She's started goin' with that shiftless Gray Wolf boy; what's she's thinkin'? You young people—all mixed up! Ja!"

I'd bent, picked up an empty bacon package and scooped the dust into it, now I moved to the spattered plastic trash can and dropped it in. But my thoughts reverted to my times with Eva. Within me images swirled, like a mountain stream, clear and crystal, flowing down from the Montana Big Horn heights.

"Hahoo, Val," interrupted Hilda, as she plopped another slab of fry bread on a red plastic server. "You're goin' to be fine."

I walked to the stove, leaned over and snitched a piece of fried bread, jumping back when Hilda swung a floured hand at me. She laughed and continued to rush her verbal tribe of brave words around me. "White man's ways is crazy. You know..." She drew circles near her head with a pudgy forefinger and laughed. Then she hot-potatoed the plate-sized fried bread into an enameled tin dish. "You think white folk in this village will help their own kind—No! Why I went and lent the Bigalows, who run the trading post, some money and you know David 'n I don't got much—why we don't got money to get eggs and milk next week—but 'cause their boy was sick. You think the other whites on the ranches over toward Jimtown would help—No! They're too busy, busy, busy!"

She slapped another huge pancake of dough into the cast iron skillet and began to fry it. I leaned back in one of the kitchen chairs and thought of Eva sitting close to me on the rocks by the silver water tower across the highway under the obsidian, starry night... six long months past.

I frowned and pushed the thought away.

Hilda talked on. "But our Indian way is the way of generosity. I remember when I was a little girl. I used to go see an old man in the village. He had a silver collection. I loved to go to his place, and I'd just stare and stare and maybe touch them a little—those pretty silver things. One day my mother made special bread for a church meeting, and I took him a dish over, and so he had to give me all his silver collection."

She looked at me very seriously. "I couldn't sit down for a week—got the worst hidin' ever when my mother gotta hold of me. And I deserved it 'cause I had given such a little thing compared to his great generosity! But that's the Indian way; a person gives a gift and the receiver shows his generosity by giving a more prized one in return. Val, ain't that what your saints used to do—give, even, their lives for others—a real sacrifice?"

*****

Friday at evening time we all piled into David's rusted grey pickup and rattled over to Lame Deer so that I could see Eva. She would be at the Indian dances at Barksdale Hall— named for a young man of a Quaker work group who had been accidentally crushed to death while constructing a community center for the Cheyenne.

I sat in the back of the Ford with the older kids—David and Hilda up front in the cab with their littlest ones, the twins. The truck whined eastward away from the Two Moons rock monument silhouetted on a bluff against the reddened sky. Their young daughter giggled the whole way to Lame Deer, trying to braid the leather fringe on the left arm of my frontier coat. I caught her several times and made a ferocious roar, extending my arms up into the air like a thin, but savage, bear. She dropped back on her skinny legs, her glowing high cheeks pinching in, showing her choke berry stained teeth. And I remembered last August when Eva and I had hiked out to the spring on her uncle and aunt's place and mouthed berries and kisses.

Barksdale Hall looked like a huge overturned feeding trough made of corrugated steel and insulated wood fiber—Quonset hut style. Every Friday night 'white' dances were held for Cheyenne young people, and for that matter other Indians, even Crow from their nearby reservation west of the Little Big Horn Battlefield. Many of the Indian youth had no interest in traditional Indian dances but listened to the latest rock n' roll and wanted to be up with what was happening in Billings, or even Los Angeles.

I walked hurriedly ahead of my Indian family. Entering the hall, I frantically scanned the groups of teens for Eva until finally I saw her standing next to a tall Indian guy by the Pepsi machine. Then came the encounter.

*****

On the frigid drive home, I huddled in the back of the pickup with the kids, covered by half a dozen blankets whose edges flapped in the subzero temperature, not nearly as cold as my inner red pumping valve. Eva hadn't even wanted to say hi to me, but finally did after Hilda had cornered her and talked. When Eva briefly came over and said we weren't 'no more', like she had written in her letter, I saw that the tattoo of my name on her arm was gone. No Pocahontas ending. Nor did I count coop, but did manage by some means to make a less-than-ashamed getaway.

About half way over the low mountain, David pulled off the highway and rumbled up a snowy jeep trail into the forest. With his headlights turned off, the dark snowy bluffs and rocky cuestas before us appeared to loom like crouching animals. He reached out and suddenly turned on the spotlight next to his side mirror and swept it across the crusted snow and scattered trees.

Commodities wouldn't be in until next week and the

family would soon be out of meat, so it was time for a deer. He lightly tapped on the back window glass so I jumped out of the back of the truck and leaned in by his open window.

David whispered to me, "Val, you should have been out there dancin' in your Cody coat, then some Indian princess would've danced with ya'."

Hilda leaned over toward us and pretended to whisper in his ear. "I think we'll just keep his coat when he goes."

Her husband smiled widely, his slight mustache barely visible in the dark. He swung the light again across the landscape, the end of the beam like a frightened mink running from the light of the countless sharp stars striking down from above.

But darkness kept chasing the searchlight. No deer tonight, for them, or for me. It was a stupid pun, but the stupidity of the thought lessened the ache inside. The hurt wasn't in my chest. Why the heart gets top billing in 'heartbreak' stories is hard to say.

On Saturday, I helped David move a pickup-full of foothill rocks to his backyard where he planned to build a very large planter for a rose garden in the spring.

*****

Sunday as I packed to leave, Hilda lumbered into the bedroom with a colorful shirt in hand. "Here, paleface, try this on. David's been eatin' too much. I got it for him, but it don't fit him in the chest." The shirt was tapered, sort of a forest green with red pin stripes—I liked it and put it on.

"You sure?" I glanced over at her. "Maybe I should wait and double check with David when he gets back from the tribal office."

"Ja, what you think I don't know my husband? Early this mornin' before sunrise, he told me to give it to you, while you were still sleepin' and dreamin' about some new Indian maiden."

I said, "Thanks, Hilda." Then I hugged her, her youngest daughter, and the twins, and said goodbye. I walked up the hill from the village to the highway toward Billings. I didn't look back at the silver water tower on the opposite bluff. The northern wind buffeted against me until my face was numb. Dumping my rucksack containing some of David and Hilda's deer jerky and fried bread, I stood on the edge of the pavement, thumb extended, my Cody fringe whipping about in the icy wind. It was the fourteenth of February, but I was no one's Valentine.

## Author's Bio: Daniel E. Wilcox

Daniel Wilcox, a former activist, teacher, and wanderer--from Nebraska to the Middle East--casts his lines out upon the world's turbulent waters and wide shores in *Counter example Poetics, Moria, Tipton Poetry Journal, The Recusant, Word Riot, The New Verse News*, etc.

His book of poetry, *Dark Energy*, was published in 2009 by Diminuendo Press.

"The Faces of Stone" set in the Middle East, appeared in The *Danforth Review* and *Danse Macabre*.

Daniel lives with a speculative novel, *The Feeling of the Earth*, and his second volume of poetry *Psalms, Yawps, and Howls*, and, last but not least;-), his wife on the central coast of California.

**Daniel on the Web:**
seaquaker.com

## After You

by:  Cathleen Thompson

Memories past love awaken
Don't know why?
Left deep hidden inside
Darken sapphire faceted moods
Ever changing mind
Glimmering gloom

Broken hearted
Wind blown hard
Shattered fragments
Finding pieces out reach
Flow of many churning rivers of tears
Should ease my fears

Teach hard life lessons
Wash my being clear
Drape fears of loss
Cloaked in shades of dreary gray
Wormed through darken rot

Mind mashed and smashed a lot
Your words of untrue
Wash down into prism of soul
Patch here patch there
Special threads to bear

Many jewel encrusted colors
Have lost their luster
Must search for light of soul

Re-weaving altering
Stitch by stitch
Healing precious self

Finding true inter beauty after you
Woven brightly shades
Happiness, future, comfort
New heart, new life sparkle
Find new love so true after you

## Author's Bio: Cathleen Thompson

Cathleen Thompson has lived in the Santa Maria, California area for 10 years, with her husband and black cat Shadow. She is a computer graphic artist and enjoys writing poetry.

## Chocolate and Roses for Molly

by: J. Diane Bechtle

Molly slammed the phone down and let out an exasperated sigh. Why did people have to be so cowardly? The hang up calls had been coming for a week now, ever since she had written the article on the war for *The Daily Messenger.*

The cowardly idiots. Anonymous crank calls. How immature. If you have something to say, say it and at least stand by it with your name.

"Just because I don't support the war, doesn't mean I don't support the troops," she muttered. "I understand they went to protect us. The war itself was a God awful mistake to begin with."

If only people would talk to one another with an open heart. Fear seemed to make people so unreasonable and defensive. She let out a sigh.

Still annoyed, Molly pushed back a strand of brunette hair from her face. As a diversion from her developing bad mood, she turned to thinking about Doug, a co-worker. He was a real hotty. She had caught him watching her many a time since he had started working at the paper two months ago. He always covered his embarrassment at being seen staring with a sheepish grin and frantic typing on his computer.

"But, I can't get caught up in an office romance," she scolded herself. "If a woman wants to get ahead in her career, she has to give two hundred percent. But," she admitted, "it is nice to have a man remind me that I am a woman.

It had been another fourteen hour workday. And she was starving. On her way to the kitchen the phone had rung.

"Not again. Should I even bother to answer it? I really don't need another game-playing dimwit."

It didn't stop, and after the tenth strident ring she gave in. "If this is another creep, I've had my quota for today."

There was a moment of silence, and she was about to slam down the phone, when she heard, "Molly, Molly it's me. Sara."

There were tears in her sister's voice. "Sara, what's the matter?"

"Oh, Molly. I planned a wonderful dinner for Steve for Valentine's Day... flowers and candles... I thought surely he would be home tonight... no matter what. Valentine's Day has always been our special day. I never dreamed he would miss it."

Sara's breathing was ragged as she spoke through her sobs. "Molly, he hasn't been home for two days. I am so worried. What if he's hurt or sick? I made a police report, but they told me he's a big boy and will find his way home before I know it. I know something's wrong. We've been arguing lately, and he's seemed under pressure at work, but he won't talk to me about it."

Molly looked longingly at the refrigerator for a moment, then said, "I'll be right over. He probably went off to pout a little if you two have been arguing. We'll sit down and figure this out together. Okay?"

Sara sniffled and there was a pause on the telephone, which Molly took for tissue time and then her sister answered, "I can't think straight at this point. Steve is usually so predictable. Disappearing is not at all his style."

"I'll be over as soon as I have a run at Burger King's drive through." She hung up the phone, and quickly gathered her keys, purse and coat.

*It is Valentine's Day. I forgot all about it. It has been so long since I and a someone male have spent time together. Human contact. Now there's a concept. With the exception of Doug, I am so busy with my job, I've even stopped noticing men.* She sighed. *Well, I wanted the glamour of a reporter's career.*

Molly rang Sara's doorbell thirty minutes later and was immediately concerned seeing her sister's drawn and worried face, red from tears.

"My, God. You look like hell."

Sara was Molly's baby sister. After their elderly parents had passed, Molly looked after her, protected her, and advised her with life's decisions.

Two years ago, she'd even checked Steve out when it became apparent Sara was falling in love with him. He was a bit too ordinary and boring for her taste, exciting as a stump. Still if he made Sara happy, that was the important thing and obviously, he was failing in that department at the moment.

Putting her things down, Molly flopped onto the couch and patted a place beside her. "Okay, girl. Just what do you think is going on here?"

"He's been coming home late from work and has been a bear. He snaps and snarls and sits in front of the TV. I've tried and tried to talk to him but he won't tell me a thing."

Molly looked at the ceiling for a moment and then said, "Where do you think he would go if he wanted to be alone and think?"

"Not to family. They're all out of state. We don't have extra money for motels or hotels. His drinking buddies would all be back slapping and trying to jolly him out of his mood, and when Steve's in a bad mood, he wants to be left alone, so that leaves them out."

Sara tucked her long legs up under her on the couch and pulled a soft, blue throw around her shoulders. Her blonde hair was in disarray and her usually sweet mouth frowned forlornly. She looked as though she wanted to disappear.

Molly's thoughts turned to how Sara looked so lovingly at Steve in happier times. *How did two people manage to stay together anyway? Sure, I get lonely when I have a moment of down time, but was it worth all the work required to keep a relationship running smoothly. I just don't know.*

"Sara, you took Steve to our folks' mountain cabin soon after you were married last year, didn't you? I almost forgot about the place it has been so long since I have had time to visit it. It would be the perfect place to hole up and re-evaluate life. Wouldn't it? It would be a perfect cave for a man to hide. It doesn't even have a telephone."

"Oh, Molly. I bet you're right. Steve loved it there. He said he felt peaceful and relaxed. We both hated to come home from that trip. He knows where the extra key is hidden, too."

"If we leave now we can be there in a couple of hours.

What do you say?"

"Let's pack a few things and go. You can borrow what you need from me so we won't have to stop at your place."

Pajamas, sweaters and toothbrushes were thrown hurriedly into a bag, and they were on the road in a few minutes.

*****

They drove in silence and soon the valley terrain gave way to foothills and then to snow-covered pines and mountains. The passing scenery was beautiful in the moonlight as the snow seemed to glow from an inner light. Occasionally snow fell off a tree branch and landed with a shimmering spray.

Sara turned to Molly with a face filled with pain. "What if he isn't at the cabin? What if something serious has happened to him? I don't know what I'd do without him."

Molly searched for a comforting response. Not finding one, she said, "But from all you've said, it makes perfect sense he'll be at the cabin. Let's trust that."

Traffic was light and soon they were pulling off the paved road onto the track that led to the cabin. Their car struggled through the snow as they slowly made their way up the drive.

"Look," Sara said, sitting up straighter and pointing at the windshield. "I think I see a light through the trees and there are tire tracks. There's a car in the driveway with a rental car logo on the back. I'm sure Steve's here."

As they parked behind the other car, the front door of the cabin opened and they could see a man's outline in the light from inside the cabin.

Sara was out of the car and running up the porch steps before Molly even had time to undo her seat belt and open her car door. By the time Molly had climbed to the porch landing, Sara and Steve were clinging to one another and crying.

Molly, feeling embarrassed, said, "Let's get inside. It 's freezing out here."

Still holding onto one another as if one of them might

vanish into thin air, Steve and Sara moved inside and settled on the sofa by the fire.

Molly followed and sat in an old leather chair across from them.

"Why are you here?" Sara said, then sniffled, "Why didn't you come home?" There was a pause, then with anger in her voice she said, "Damn it! I didn't know if you were dead or alive! I've been sick with worry. And not a word from you!"

Steve turned away with an anguished-filled face. "I'm so sorry, Sara. I was miserable. I wanted to run away and hide so no one would see me like that. Most of all you. They laid me off. Laid off. I just couldn't face you. I've let you down… all our plans and dreams… I promised you so much and…"

Sara looked as though he had slapped her in the face. "Steve, do you think so little of me that you believe I wouldn't be there for you? That I wouldn't have faith in you?" She struggled a moment to gain control over her anger then said, "There are other jobs out there. I know you'll move heaven and earth to take care of us. We can always get along on my salary for a little while until you find something. I am so shocked and disappointed you don't know I am here for good or bad. Damn you for scaring me. We're a team, you idiot."

Molly felt a rush of pride at her sister's directness. She wanted to yell 'you go, girl!' but remained silent. Besides, Sara was doing a great job all on her own.

Steve turned toward Sara and put his hand on her cheek. "I am so sorry. I should have trusted you. This relationship stuff is still new to me, and I guess I'm stuck in the old fashioned notion that a man takes care of his woman. My father never missed a day at work and lived his life to take care of us. He was always the strong one. Losing my job… I felt like a complete failure. I couldn't stand to have you to see me like that."

Molly looked around the cabin wishing there was somewhere she could go, but the one large room and open sleeping loft offered no such luxury. The bathroom walls were paper thin so no help there. So instead, she squirmed in her chair.

Sara and Steve sat quietly and stared into the fire.

At last Sara said, " I guess it's the nature of relationships to misunderstand one another. We create imaginary stories about what the other person is feeling, or ascribe motives for what they are doing out of our own fears or desires. It's a learning process to begin to ask the other person what they meant, or why they did something. It takes courage to risk an answer we might not like or not understand."

She paused and then went on. "I made up all sorts of things about your disappearance… another woman who was prettier than me or you had some horrible; deadly disease or the truth about you was you were just an unreliable, inconsiderate boob."

"Well, the boob part is close. I am so sorry I put you through this worry."

Sara smiled. "Let's agree never to assume anything about the other. That if we have an upset about anything, and I mean anything, we'll sit down and talk about it. Agreed? Otherwise, we are doomed to drama. Look at the last three days."

"Sara, I'm so lucky to have you in my life."

Sara responded, "Yes, you *are* very lucky!" Then with another smile she said, "The roads are too icy to drive home tonight. Shall we go upstairs?"

*****

Molly stood and threw on another log, poking until it caught, and then returned to her chair. *How did my baby sister get so smart?*

Her thoughts turned back to the war. Misunderstanding, that was the root of it, just like Sara and Steve. Assuming the other person has all the negative aspects, that we don't want to acknowledge are a part of us. And because it's not acknowledged, we project it onto others. Once we do that, we have *carte blanche* to attack what we really abhor in ourselves. She nodded. *My next article will be about relationships, and the same mistakes we make in them.*

She thought about an incident. It illustrated misunderstandings in a nutshell. She was in college and still living at home. A young man, David, in whom she was interested, had come over for the evening. They were in the beginning of their relationship with one another. Sitting in the living room together, David asked for a glass of water, and she told him to help himself. They went round and round for several minutes, he asking her to get the water and Molly telling him he was welcome to get it himself.

Noticing their obvious energy in the interchange, they finally talked about what was going on underneath his simple request for a glass of water. It was then they saw that each of them had an agenda that had little to do with water, and a lot to do with hopes and expectations for a relationship.

She wanted to let David know he was welcome in her home and could feel comfortable there, so she told him he could help himself. David, however, was asking for the water to see if Molly was the type of woman who would enjoy catering to a man.

Good God! No wonder relationships seemed so impossibly crazy at times.

Molly thought of the crank telephone calls she had been getting since the publication of her article on the war. *They feel as frustrated as I do about the situation. I don't have to like their methods but I can understand their pain.* With that thought, the calls suddenly seemed less upsetting.

She moved to the sofa and pulled a pillow over her head to muffle the sighs, whispers and giggles drifting down from the loft. Nothing like spending a Valentine's night alone on a lumpy sofa to promote change.

Molly thought of Doug at the office. She had to admit, he was cute, single, funny and straight. A rarity. He gave Molly a huge, inviting smile whenever they crossed paths but she was always in a rush to make some deadline and hurried past with only a curt nod.

She smiled. *I think I'll give Doug a chance next time we meet. I'm pretty sure I can remember how to flirt. Just acknowledging I'm lonely and need more than a byline for warmth is the first step. Less work and more love is my new affirmation. I'll slow down my life and remember to listen for what is underneath. I just saw how talking can save a relationship. Maybe someday it can even stop wars.*

Molly groaned. I never thought I'd windup spending Valentine's Day with Sara and Steve. *Next Valentine's Day I'm going to have my own hot date.* She let out a wistful sigh as she envisioned red roses and chocolates just for her.

## Author's Bio: J. Diane Bechtle

Diane Bechtle, born and raised in Redding, California, lived 42 years in the Bay Area and three years in the foothills of the Gold Country above Stockton before settling on the Central Coast. She joined the Word Wizards to polish her book, *A Moose in the Room*, which chronicles her psychic experiences and spiritual journey. There she found a group of fascinating, creative writers with much to say. Since then, *A Moose in the Room*, now known as, *I know Something and So Do You*, has been published by Coastal Dunes Publishing.

## The Lady in the Valentine Sweater

by: Maggie Pucillo

Ruth stepped cautiously along the sidewalk, picking up then placing each foot as if testing the tensile strength of the concrete and the integrity of the ground beneath. She stopped and looked carefully both ways when she came to the driveway of the Japanese restaurant. She stepped more quickly until she was on the other side, then peered around. She walked to the BMW parked at the curb across from the health club, opened the passenger side, got in and closed the door.

A man sweeping near the dumpster glanced at the woman when she opened the car door. He noted her unusual combination of sweat pants, nightgown and rubber boots and a large purple sweater with bright red hearts. He wondered about people who didn't lock their cars, made a mental note to pick up a valentine bouquet for his wife on his way home, and returned to his work.

As the lady settled herself she glanced around at the sumptuous interior of the big car. *Oh. This isn't my car. Okay, I just need to sit down and rest for a moment. I haven't taken a walk all week; guess I'm a little out of condition....*

\*\*\*\*\*

She had risen from bed as usual that morning. Her nighttime caretaker, Sadie, helped her with warm-up exercises, guiding the long arms and legs through a set of range-of-motion moves. Sadie laid out clothes for the day, helped with dressing as needed, arranged Ruth's medications and supplements, pressed a kiss on the papery cheek and said, "Your day lady will be here any minute. I have a doctor's appointment. Will you be okay on your own for a bit, Ruthie?"

"Of course. You go. Remember to give your sweetheart a kiss. It's Valentine's Day today.

"Well, so it is. Have a nice day, dear," she said and was gone.

Ruth moved into the bathroom for the morning wash up, congratulating herself on still having most of her own teeth. She peered into the mirror as she applied her moisturizer and the touch of blush and lipstick she always wore. Her long, narrow face and pale blue eyes looked back at her the same as they had yesterday and the day before that.

*But today's my birthday.* She smiled at herself and brushed back her wavy silver hair and clipped it at her neck. Then she went to the kitchen for coffee and fruit. Just as Ruth poured her first cup of coffee, the phone rang.

"Good morning, Ruth. This is Denise at the agency. How are you?"

"Good morning, Denise. I'm doing well for being seventy-seven years old today. It's my birthday, you know. How are you, dear?"

"Happy birthday, Ruth, I'm just fine. I'm calling to let you know we've had to make a little change for today. I just got a call from your daytime lady. She's had a car accident and won't be in. I've sent Helen as a substitute. You remember Helen, don't you?"

"Oh yes, Helen…"

"She'll be there soon. You have your coffee and wait for her. I'll call her cell and let her know it's your birthday. How does that sound to you?"

"We'll have a little party. Thank you for calling. Bye now."

*****

Denise ended the call and turned to her assistant. "I hope Helen finds the address and arrives soon. Ruth tells me it's her birthday, again. She thinks every holiday is her birthday. Today is Valentine's Day, not her birthday."

"I remember her. The family has been with the agency for years, haven't they?"

"Yes, they were some of our first customers. Ruth called on us for help with her parents toward the end of their lives, and then decided she wanted a 'maid' for herself. The team that's with her now has worked there for, oh, about fifteen years, I think. It's an interesting story. The family was Pasadena pioneers, old money from back east."

"Yes, that's where I remember the name. The Hunt Club, right?"

"Right. The grandparents were among the founding members, I think. The parents were quite something and it's a great love story. They fell in love in elementary school, and married the summer after college graduation. He came home from the office for lunch each day, just to see her. On full-moon nights they had dinner on the verandah and danced in the moonlight, or so the story goes."

"Now that's a Valentine Day story with real romance. Doesn't Ruth have a brother somewhere?"

"Yes, somewhere," Denise said. "He left home for college and never came back. I think he was at the parent's funeral. Doesn't seem to be involved with his sister at all. Ruth never speaks of him. He sends a gift basket to our office once in a while, 'thanks for everything, blah blah blah'. He's kind of a creep, as I remember. The family's attorney, Charles Ralphson, takes care of all the business."

"So, poor, old Ruth is pretty much on her own?"

"Well, yes she is; but she's not poor, believe me. Worth millions, you know, and not all that old either, only seventy-seven. I hope I outlive her. We've taken good care of her for a long time. Next home visit, I want you to come along and meet her. She's a dear soul."

\*\*\*\*\*

Ruth put the receiver back and gazed out the kitchen window, coffee forgotten for the moment. She was lost in the past remembering—but not exactly—a long ago Valentine's Day. The Valentine's dance at her school prompted her to invite a boy from the neighborhood. On the way home, the boy produced a bottle of brandy, which set the tone for the melee that followed. She fought him off, but the attempted rape shattered Ruth's delicate confidence. After a year of daily psychotherapy, Ruth renounced the world and entered a convent.

She returned to the family home years later to look after her aging and ill parents. In the business of returning to the world and arranging for their care, Ruth sometimes exhibited unusual behavior, which was viewed as eccentricity. Her early onset Alzheimer's went undiagnosed.

Her parents were true soul mates, very much in love, and each Valentine's Day was an event. She remembered little of those times, but the red roses blooming in tubs on her patio echoed celebrations held in days gone by.

*Well, enough of that. I'll have something to eat and take a little walk, I think. I wonder where the maid is? Oh well, guess I'm still able to fix myself a nice tuna sandwich.*

She spooned tuna from the can onto rye crackers, bit into one, then wandered off to prepare for her walk. She pulled on a pair of sweat pants, then a nightgown over her dress, and stepped out onto the patio. A pair of ancient gardening boots stood by the garage door. She sat on a bench, slipped them on over her house shoes, and went out the side gate.

*It's a little chilly, maybe I should go back for my sweater—oh, there it is.* Two doors from her house a sweater hung on a mailbox. It was brilliant purple with large red hearts crowded over the entire garment. *Good, now I'm warm. I think I'll just walk to the corner and back.*

The Hastings Ranch development in Pasadena, built in the fifties, featured double sized lots. Mature trees and large gardens isolated the sprawling ranch style and French colonial homes from one another. Neighbors seldom glimpsed each other for months at a time, and no one saw the lady as she made her way along. The streets curved, continuing down the small mesa to the commercial district below. Helen, the substitute from the agency, rushing to find the address, took no note of the tall, thin woman stepping slowly along the sidewalk.

*****

"Oh, hello there, is this your car? It's beautiful, isn't

it?" Ruth said to the man who opened the driver's side door.

"What are you doing in my car?" the man said. "Who are you?" He threw his bag in the backseat and slid into the driver's seat.

"Oh, don't worry, I didn't touch anything. I'm Helen, I mean, Ruth. I just needed to sit and rest a while. Your beautiful car was right here so I thought—"

"Look lady, I don't care what you thought. What are you nuts, just getting into cars whenever you feel like it? Out, out. I'm late for a meeting and I don't have time to listen to you. Out."

He reached across her and flung open the door, muttering to himself. Ruth gathered her nightgown around her and swung her legs out the door. She stood and slammed the door.

"Listen young man, I don't care for your tone, and furthermore—" Her words trailed off as he put the car in gear and sped away.

"What a grouch, and on my birthday, too," she said and turned to the worker who was now hosing down the space at the rear of the restaurant.

"Oh, your birthday today?" he said. "Valentine's Day also. Your sweater is very, uh, colorful. My boss, he gives people free tea and cookies for birthday, you like to come inside and have tea?"

"Why, yes I would, thank you," she said.

The man turned off the hose, tossed it aside, wiped his hands on his pants and offered her his arm. "Come with me, we go around to front door."

He congratulated her on her birthday and handed the lady off to the hostess with a quick explanation, then went through the dining room and into the kitchen. He stuck his head into the office and spoke to the secretary at the desk. "I think that lady in trouble. Kim giving her tea and cookie now. I think lady is lost. You go see, maybe call someone for her?" and went out the back door to continue his work.

Ruth sat at the sushi bar sipping hot tea. She adjusted her sweater and sat a little straighter as Kim put a small plate of delicate cookies in front of her.

"So, it's your birthday today", Kim said. "How lovely. You're a little Valentine, aren't you? Your sweater is beautiful."

"Oh, thank you dear, it's kind of you to arrange this little party. Why, I remember birthdays in the past when we would celebrate with roses and wine and a lovely dinner. The chandelier lit up the whole room and made the crystal and silver just shine. My Stephen was great for celebrating my birthday with me."

"I'm sure it was lovely. Oh, would you excuse me for just a moment? My manager is signaling me, be right back."

The manager hissed behind his hand, "Keep her talking. I've called the police, told them we have an elderly wanderer here. They're going to send a car over to pick her up, but it may be a while."

"I'll do what I can, but I've got to move her to a booth. The lunch crowd will be arriving any time now."

"Fine, just keep her here."

Kim turned to smooth her hair and check her make up in the mirror; and when she returned to the counter, the lady was gone. She went out the front door and looked around. The lady in the Valentine sweater seemed to have vanished into thin air.

Ruth turned right when she left the restaurant, and turned right again when she came to Orange Grove Boulevard. She made her way a little more quickly now.

*The tea and cookies have given me some pep. I think I'll just walk to the corner. My, there's a lot of traffic here.*

Her nightgown swirled as the passing trucks and cars sped up to catch the light. A truck with Salvation Army signage on the side saluted her with a jaunty beep of the horn as they passed and Ruth waved back. She was now in front of the theater complex and stopped to look at the marquees.

A group of high school students dressed in full gothic regalia lingered near the curb. "Check it, the old dame is strutting it. Hey, snug duds, lady," one called out.

"Oh, this is my new gown. Do you think it goes with

the sweater?" Ruth said. "I've just come out for a walk. How are you today? Are you going to the show?"

The group moved toward her, surrounded her, laughing and talking among themselves. They recognized her as one of their own with social courage enough to blaze her own path, at least in matter of dress.

"Hey lady, you're the show. What's up, you alone?" The circle of teenagers moved closer around her.

"You expecting a flood, lady? Check out the boots. Dude."

"The sweater is cool, babe," a girl said and moved to put her arm around Ruth's shoulders. "It matches pretty well. Where's your purse?"

"Oh, I have a wonderful purse at home," Ruth said. "My darling Wesley gave it to me one year for a birthday present. It's alligator skin, quite sophisticated. A dark green, much like it was when the alligator wore it," Ruth said and laughed. "You would have liked my Ralphie He loved to wear black, and he also liked his boots. I see you all have quite large boots on today."

"Dude," one said, "what have we got here?"

"Yes, Ralphie gave me many gifts over the years. One time we made a little wager between ourselves. I don't recall now what it was, but the loser had to take the winner to dinner. Well, I won the bet and my sweetie flew us to San Francisco for dinner at the Top of the Mark. Isn't that something?"

Significant looks passed between members of the group lingering in the back. One of them spoke up. "Say lady, it looks like you aren't really dressed to be out. Why don't I take you home?"

"Jack, leave her alone," another said.

"You're not taking this lady anywhere," the girl next to Ruth said.

"Hey, bitch, mind your own business. I'll drive her home if I want to," Jack said and grabbed at the girl.

"Just when did you get so helpful, Jack? Get back," she yelled and went for his throat. A black clad vampire clone lifted Jack by the collar and hissed at him to shut up. Another grabbed and held the girl as the two escalated into fury, spitting and growling.

"Now you wait just a minute. What do you think you're doing?" Ruth had found her voice and stepped between the combatants. "You children are acting like animals. Shoo! Stop it right this minute. Mind your manners. I want you to go inside and watch your show. Or go back to school, that's where you should be anyway. I'll be calling your parents as soon as I get back to my office. Now go on, go on." Her unexpected intervention and tone of authority seemed to strike a chord with the group and they dispersed, muttering to themselves. She walked behind them, shooing them toward the theatre as though they were a flock of wayward geese.

Standing on the sidewalk, she watched the oddly stylish group disappear into the theatre lobby. She continued walking, still on her walk 'down to the corner', a tall, slight, gray haired lady in a valentine sweater.

*****

The couple in the custom Cadillac in the far corner of the parking lot watched Ruth's approach with surprise. Germane wasn't used to old white ladies approaching his flash ride, especially when he had one of his girls with him.

"Here, fix me and git up, sum'one's comin," he said and pushed her away. "Shit girl, do sumpthin' wit' yo dress, git up now." He made to slap at her, but Betty Lou was used to his ways and grabbed a towel lying on the seat, wiped her mouth and pulled her dress down as he zipped his fly.

"What is this, senior citizen's day, shit? What that ol' lady want wit me?" he whined.

"Just relax, daddy. I'll deal with this," Betty Lou said. She knew Germane would be in a foul temper, but with a little hit off his pipe to relax, he'd be ready for anything.

She looked forward to her night off, and didn't want to deal with his moods, as she thought of them. Her life was tough enough, and his moods often involved violence.

"Hi there, kids. Say, I wonder..." Ruth began.

147

Betty Lou got out of the car, keeping an eye on her 'agent' as she walked around to where Ruth stood. "Good morning, mother," she said, "What do you wonder?"

"Well, I was just wondering which way Hastings Ranch Drive is, I think I've gotten turned around."

Betty Lou saw Germane lean over and light the crack pipe. *Damn, I hope he calms down.* "I think it's that way, about a block or two." She heard the crackling, smelled the foul smoke drifting out the open window and began to walk the old lady away from the car. *Can't get too far away or he'll take too much and then it'll be shit for lunch.*

"Let me show you, come on." The two started toward the street. "That's a beautiful sweater you've got on. Right, today is Valentine's day."

"Yes, it is. Is that your boyfriend in the car?" Ruth asked.

"Uh, well, I guess so. Yes, that's my boyfriend."

"I hope he takes you out for dinner and is sweet to you on this special day."

"It's my day off. That is, uh... maybe we'll have dinner. He's not feeling too well, right now."

"Oh, I know how it is when they're sick. My Roberto had the flu one year on Valentine's Day, but he still—" She broke off as the car door slammed and Germane's angry voice interrupted.

"Ah, the flu. Yes, I think my boyfriend has the flu. I've got to go now. He'll need his medicine, you understand."

Germane grabbed Betty Lou by the arm. "Git back in the car, right now. You got some bid'ness to git to, girl."

"Oh now, that's not the way to treat her. Let her go," Ruth said, her voice rising.

He pushed Betty Lou hard and she took a few running steps to keep from falling. "C'mon Germane, please. I'm goin', I'm goin'. Don't—"

"You don' tell me, bitch," he said, and then turned to Ruth. "And you, you ol' bag, who you think you talkin' to? She mine and I be talkin' any way I want," and he raised his hand as if to slap her.

Ruth saw his eyes widen as he looked from her face to something behind her, and he suddenly became very still. She smelled his body odor, rank and stinking as he broke into a sweat. His eyes, the whites yellowed and lined with red, mirrored rage; yet he dropped his arm and backed slowly away from her, his face stiff with fear. After a few steps, he turned and ran toward the car. In seconds he threw the door open and accelerated out of the lot.

Ruth watched this drama in awe. She was aware of a presence just behind her, and turned, expecting to see a police officer. Instead she looked into the face of a tall, tousle-coated gray dog. The dog's tail waved slowly, her eyes gleaming and serene. She bowed her head briefly; and when it rose, Ruth saw a heart- shaped tag with the name "Angel" on a collar about the long neck.

The dog walked with Ruth to a nearby concrete planter, lowered then raised her head once more and walked away behind her. Ruth sat, stunned by the events. She barely registered Germane's violence, but the dog's air of compassion left her with a vague concern for her whereabouts.

*So many folks I've never met before are out today. And the lovely dog... I'm still on my walk to the corner, aren't I? Silly one, of course you are.*

The Japanese restaurant, a health club, a day spa, specialty grocery market and office buildings surrounded the vast parking lot where she sat.

*Well then, that's as may be; but I need the restroom now.* She stood, a bit unsteady, but walked with determination toward the 'Jeunesse Doree Day Spa'.

"Good morning, madam. How may I help you?" the woman at the desk greeted her. "Beautiful day, isn't it, how are you? My name is Yolande. You are a member of the club?"

"Oh, dear yes," Ruth said. "My family has charter membership, as a matter of fact. My grandfather was a founding member, you know."

"Oh, really. We're so pleased you could join us today."

The week before Yolande had had a meeting with the

149

spa manager. He told her of a complaint he had received regarding her tone of voice as she responded to a wealthy client.

"Here in our Hastings Ranch store we want to be careful and treat everyone as though they're The Queen. Now, now—I know what you're going to say, I spoke to the woman who called and mentioned your name."

"Then you know how unpleasant and pushy...." Yolande began.

"Indeed. She is, how to say, *nouveau riche* and completely unaware of how grating her manner appears," the manager continued. "Nevertheless, we treat each and every customer in the same way; impeccable manners and sincere graciousness, always. You'll find that will take you a long way in your career, dear."

And Yolande heeded her manager's advice. *Hm-mmm, even though she's dressed like a bag lady, she is The Queen. She will have the best, as always.*

"And what did you say your name was?"

"I'm Helen. Excuse me, I mean Sister." Ruth laughed happily and patted the receptionist's arm. "Just say Sister Maria Dominica, that will do."

Ruth's composure slipped a bit at the exchange. *What was that all about?* she asked herself. *Really.*

"Yes, Sister. Right away. Collette, this is Sister Maria Dominica. Please escort her to a dressing room in the Violet Section."

"Very well, then, Sister. Will you come with me?"

Collette led Ruth to a spacious dressing room and left with, "Just slip into the robe, and I'll be right back."

\*\*\*\*\*

Ruth sat in one of the French Regency armchairs, took off her boots, leaned back and wiggled her toes. She looked around her, wondering where the restroom might be. Just then Collette popped her head in.

"Oh, I see you've removed your, ah, footwear. Shall we

begin with the pedicure?"

"A pedicure will be delightful, but first I must use the restroom."

"Of course, just through here. This is a private suite, so take your time, cherie.

Ruth breathed a sigh of relief as Colette left her alone in the bathroom. *Ah, even a bidet. At last....*

When she finished, she washed her hands, luxuriating in the French milled herbal soap, used the wrapped toothbrush she found on the shelf above the sink, and ended by rinsing her mouth with the mouthwash.

*This is lovely, all the niceties of home. Wonder what's in here?*

She opened a door and stepped into a massage parlor. The lights were dimmed, a small fountain played in the corner, and a delightful scent filled the air.

*Perfect, I'll just lie down and take a little nap, then return home.*

The warm flannel sheet wrapped snugly around the Valentine sweater; and as she adjusted the pillow under her head and closed her eyes, she murmured, *he kissed my throat and called me Beauty.*

The masseuse tapped softly on the door and entered to find Ruth snoring lightly. "I'll return in a few moments. Enjoy your rest," she whispered and slipped out.

When Eloise, the masseuse, returned for the fifth time, she found Ruth awake, sitting up on the table and looking around her, her sweater on her lap.

"Did Madam have a lovely rest?"

"*Oui, certainmant*," Ruth said. "You know," she began, as Eloise bustled around the room collecting massage oils and adjusting the volume of the music. "My Clifford entertained me one evening and spoke only French throughout. He met me at the door dressed in a white shirt and bow tie with a towel over his arm. He handed me a glass of champagne and led me to a perfumed bath. There were lilies and the room was filled with lovely, flickering candles." She gestured with elegant hands, encompassing a large room that glimmered in her past.

"Ah, what a romantic he was, eh?" Eloise said.

"After the bath, we had dinner on the terrace, and we danced between courses. It was my birthday, as it is today. It was so lovely."

"What a delightful memory, Madam."

"Oh, yes. My darling is with the angels now, you know, but he's left me with so many loving souvenirs," Ruth said.

"What enchantment," Eloise said. "Would Madam care to disrobe now and we can get on…"

"What?" Ruth shrieked. She was at once surrounded with memories of endless, dark halls and small rooms. Women robed in black clustered near her, and she felt very alone and vulnerable. Terror and a childish fear of exposure and ridicule filled her.

"I absolutely will not," she yelled. "You filthy pigs are all alike. I've told mother about this, many times, but she would not believe me. Disgusting degenerates, all of you."

Ruth scrambled off the table, grabbed her sweater and rushed out. She passed through the bathroom muttering, and slammed the door behind her. Finding her boots in the sitting room, she slipped into them quickly. She ran down the short hall, casting quick looks over her shoulder as she passed through the reception area.

She screamed, "I'll tell mother about this, and she'll not send any more checks to this contemptible place. I'm leaving and you'll never see me again."

"What…." The masseuse joined the women at the desk, and the three stood looking out the front door, astonished. Ruth cast an anxious look in their direction, turned to the left, and walked stoically toward Orange Grove Boulevard.

*****

Ruth was joined by a small group of Latino nannies as she waited for the light at the corner.

"What delightful children. My, they look healthy and strong. You must be very good mothers," Ruth said as they crossed the boulevard together.

"*No, Señora, somos niñeras. Esos niños son muy jovenes y las madres son trabajando*," one said, as she passed and began the climb up the steep hill. She spoke to the woman who walked next to her, and they both looked over their shoulder at the same moment, their eyes sweeping from Ruth's valentine sweater to her boots. One covered a smile with her hand.

The woman closest to Ruth spoke, translating the others' remark. "We are not the mothers of these children. We are the nannies, *las niñeras*. The children are very young and their mothers are at work. And you, *señora?*"

"I live near. I'm out for my morning walk. Do you and your *campañeras* live here with the families?"

"Some of us do. I am old; my children are grown with families of their own. I stay here during the week and go to my house on the weekends."

The group was spread out now, with less conversation. The younger women were farther up the hill; some had turned off along the way. Ruth and her interpreter were the last to reach the top.

"Do you need help, *señora?* I can walk home with you if you like."

"I'm well, thank you. Just on my way home now."

"We meet here each day to walk *los niños*. Join us if you like. *Adios*," she said and, with a wave, turned onto her street.

The climb up the hill had been strenuous, and Ruth was tired and thirsty. She moved to the side of the street and sat on a low stone wall to catch her breath. It was quiet here, the sounds of traffic and commerce vague and far away below on the boulevard. Birds swirled above her in the oak canopy chirping and calling. A ground squirrel peeped out at her from under a hedge.

*I feel as though I could just lie down and sleep.*

And that's what she did. She moved around the corner where there was an opening in the hedge and a hidden patch of lawn. She curled up in her nightgown, rolled the valentine sweater for a pillow, and drifted off.

*****

Ruth awakened slowly and lifted her head. Footsteps shuffled leaves nearby and small twigs crunched. A loud, snuffling breath and a somehow familiar smell came to her. It was completely dark, except for a fingernail moon and pinpoint stars. She heard sprinklers hiss to life and stood quickly, grabbing her valentine sweater from the ground. She clutched the hedge to stop the dizziness she felt from standing so quickly.

*Well, what in the world. I had a good rest, but night has fallen and I'm absolutely starved. I've missed dinner, no doubt.*

The sounds of crackling leaves stopped, and she heard something between a wheeze and a cough to her right. Ignoring the sound for the moment, she stretched, and still holding to the hedge, looked around. Up a small rise she saw a large house; dim lights glimmered upward from a pool; smaller lights outlined a spreading olive tree.

*All right, may as well get this over with. There's someone or something standing about three feet to my right. Whatever it is, is calm. I'm sure there's no danger.*

She turned her head slowly and looked into the face of a dog, shoulders the same distance from the ground as hers. The Irish wolfhound whuffed softly and walked toward Ruth, tail wagging tentatively.

"My stars, it's you, Angel," Ruth said, "You're absolutely lovely, aren't you?"

The shaggy head lowered a bit as if in a bow, the heart shaped tag gleaming in the dim light. Ruth reached out her closed hand and the dog stepped closer, lowering her muzzle to Ruth's hand. The world seemed to stop spinning for an instant and two souls met.

"Well then, dear, where are we? It's very late, or very early, I'm not just sure. Are you working, keeping others away from your home? Or is this your home?"

The great hound whuffed and walked up toward the

house. Ruth followed slowly.

"You know, being out in the dark like this reminds me of the day my James bought his new tractor. That was when we were farming in Minnesota." Ruth paused, looked around. "Although this place doesn't look at all like Minnesota."

"He had been saving for years, it seemed, and finally the big day came. A neighbor had driven him into town. He drove the tractor to my place. It was dark as it is now, when he arrived in the yard, the same moon in the west."

Lost in her musings, Ruth sat on the lawn next to where the hound stood and draped the valentine sweater around its neck. She shrugged her arms out of the nightgown, and arranged it around her neck as a scarf.

"I was hungry, as I am now, by the way. I looked out the window and saw a sight I'll never forget. Colored lights twinkled around the top of the tractor's cab, and I heard music playing. He ran to the house and in the door quick as a wink and wrapped me in his arms."

The dog lay on its side, head near Ruth. "We were laughing and twirling; and he suddenly stopped and smiled into my eyes and said, "Come for a ride with me?""

"Of course," I said and reached for my sweater; by the way, it was one just like you have.

"We drove out onto the road and went up toward the Olson place. Wonderful music played, classical guitar, I think, a very clean, calm sound. We stopped at the bottom of the hill by the Dwane Johnson place. There's a little creek there, you remember."

Now the hound was stretched out completely, groaning softly, stretching for a comfortable spot. Ruth reached over, rubbed an ear and went on. "I won't give you all the details now, but there was champagne, yes, really. And a single red rose in a small vase. Later, we got down from the tractor and danced a small dance in the road. Yes, right there by the creek. Isn't that a good story? All on the day he bought his tractor. It was a Farmall, if I remember correctly."

*****

Ruth's brother, Carl, was exiting the 605-freeway north onto the 210 west, and talking to Denise from the home care agency. "Let's go over this again, slowly and sequentially. Start from the beginning. I'm on the freeway."

"Of, course, sir. This morning our employee, Maureen, was in a car accident. Maureen is the woman who works with your sister on the day shift. Because of the accident, it was necessary for her to take the day off. We called and spoke to your sister immediately, of course, and dispatched a substitute. Your sister wouldn't have been without a caretaker for more than fifteen minutes at the very most, sir."

Carl bit down on his cigarette, and bared his teeth. He checked the mirrors and settled into the third lane from the left. He adjusted the seat of the big BMW, slid lower into the leather, and wished he were still in his office.

*Why me? Isn't there someone else they could have called? I thought they were supposed to call—*

"Sir, are you there," Denise said.

"Yes, I'm here." *Here on this damned freeway.* "You contacted me at 10:30 this morning. I was in a meeting. You told me the substitute arrived and found the house empty. I left as soon as my meeting finished. I'm nearly to Pasadena, and it's almost 5PM now. It was a hellish drive from Capistrano, by the way. I want to hear you tell me this has all been a mistake and that my sister is in her home taking a nap or something."

"We've contacted the authorities and one of our employees has been at the house all day. We've been searching the neighborhood since 8AM, but there's been no sign of her. I'm sorry to disappoint you."

Carl threw the burning cigarette out the window and ground his teeth.

"I'll be at your office shortly. I'm thinking perhaps my attorney will be with me. You may want to call your legal. This is one hundred percent unacceptable. Good bye, madam."

*My God, who are these people, can't even keep track of one dimwitted old lady. I need a drink.* Carl took the next off ramp and headed for a cocktail lounge he remembered.

\*\*\*\*\*

"Those were the days, my dear," Ruth said to the dog. "Well, it's time for us to get up and doing. Come, let's find something to eat."

The sky in the east was beginning to brighten as the two walked carefully up the rise to the patio.

"My stars, look at this." Ruth threw up her hands. "Is this what you've been guarding so well all night, my dear?"

The three pillar candles guttered in their jars and threw a feeble, flickering light over the table. The remains of a simple feast—mixed grill on a tray with vegetables on the side, salad in a large wooden bowl and a basket of bread—sat almost untouched. Three empty bottles of wine stood upside down in a bucket. Items of clothing sketched a trail on the deck toward an enclosed patio at the end of the house.

"I think the two of us can finish this up quite easily. It's been a long time since I've eaten. I believe I will start with a piece of fish and some of these lovely potatoes. Will you have chicken or beef? I can serve you some of each, if you like."

She carved from the large platter and placed it on the chair next to her. The dog sniffed it all carefully and chose small bites, one at a time. Ruth picked the skin from the salmon and chose a piece of bread. She drank from the water glass and finished up with a small plate of salad just as the sun rose.

"Will you wait for me here? I'm just going to step into the camellias for a moment. I'll be right with you."

She walked slowly back toward the table, her hands patting her hair into place, then dusting off her shoulders. The early morning sun showed her face calm, a slight smile at the corners of her mouth.

"I do hope the birdies won't mind, but I used their bath to freshen up. Thank you for waiting, my dear. I'm sorry to say good-by to you, but I must be going now. You have been a delightful companion and I will miss you."

The big dog walked solemnly at her side and sat when Ruth stepped out onto the sidewalk.

"Don't be blue, dear. We'll meet again," she said and waved as she turned. "Oh, my sweater." The dog listened and looked deep into her eyes, then turned and walked to where they'd slept side by side and picked up the sweater. She walked to Ruth and sat down in front of her. Ruth took the valentine sweater and kissed the dog on the muzzle, before turning and walking away.

*****

Carl awoke to a tangled bed, his head an overripe melon. He was in a suite at the Hilton in Arcadia.

*Who knew so many of my old mates were still here in town? God, my head.* He made his way to the bathroom, but stopped short of the door when he heard the shower.

*Now what?* He smelled coffee, detoured to the kitchen, poured a cup, and lit a cigarette. *I think there was something said about Valentine's Day about the time we got last call—wonder who I celebrated with?*

He stood in the doorway, drinking coffee and smoking. When the bathroom door opened, he sputtered and nearly dropped the cup.

"Dude," the boy smiled and walked toward him, toweling his long blond hair. "Whoa, way to celebrate, eh? How'za coffee?"

*Oh, man...* Carl whined. *I thought the therapist said I wasn't going to do that anymore. Shit.*

"You up for some breakfast, cutie?" the boy said, and dropped the towel.

"Uh, no I don't think so," Carl said. "Got some business I've got to catch up with, but hey, nice time. I'll call when I get back in town, eh? How you doin'? Need some money for breakfast?"

"Dude," the boy said and Carl fumbled for his wallet.

By the time Carl reached the home care agency's office, he was settled in his bad mood, partly because he'd fallen off the wagon last night and partly because he wouldn't be back in his office for hours. He had left a message for the family's attorney and decided he'd fake it with Denise. *Make a lot of noise and back her into a corner and I'll get what I want.*

The meeting with Denise didn't actually go as he had planned, and two hours later he was in his attorney's waiting room. His sister still hadn't been located. *I'll sue the pants off that woman. Who is she to tell me what my sister needs?*

After two cups of bad coffee, the administrative assistant finally showed him into the office. The man rose from behind the desk to greet him. "Carl, how are you? We haven't seen you in Pasadena for years."

"Charles, good to see you. I know, long time no see. I'm comfortable in Capistrano, and you're doing a good job with the family's affairs. You don't need me. And I'm very busy, business is booming."

"Thank you, have a seat. Coffee?"

"God, no. Listen, I've got a problem with the agency that's been taking care of Ruth. They seem to have lost her, and I've lost two days at my office already to come up here. I'm fed up and—"

"Now settle down, Carl. We were notified this morning. My assistant has made inquiries. We're all working on this. I don't see that the agency is at fault, unless there are some mitigating circumstances I don't know about. We'll talk this through. How about a Bloody Mary? You look like you could use one."

Carl found himself in the unfamiliar position of being told what to do. He leaned back in the chair and watched Charles prepare the drink, hand it to him, and leave the room in silence. Carl swallowed about half the drink and sighed as equilibrium, of a sort, returned. He leaned back and recalled the blond with a towel in his hand.

*****

Ruth smelled coffee and heard music coming from a garage. She drew even with the property and peered up the driveway. There were five men, some with coffee cups, some tuning instruments, playing scales and chatting.

She thought twice, then made her way up the driveway.

"Good morning, I'm Ruth. The coffee smells wonderful."

"Morning. C'mon up," one called. He gave the twelve string a final tweak and put it on the table, then walked to the front of the garage.

"Oop, what's this?" he said quietly to the bass player who joined him, then, "Here, let me help you, the driveway is steep right here."

The first thing the two men saw was Ruth's smile, then her erratic ensemble, twisted and stained by the night spent outdoors. Her hair was tangled and over her shoulder, the valentine sweater showed a hint of drool with pieces of grass here and there. In the back someone whistled the first two bars of *My Funny Valentine*.

"How are you this fine morning, dear?" Harry escorted Ruth to the table, seated her and said, "Now, do you take cream or sugar or brandy in your coffee?"

"Oh, my," Ruth said. "I think just a little cream if you have any." She felt welcome, but flustered, being surrounded by men. "I'm returning from my walk. It seems an age since I had my morning coffee. Thank you so much."

"Enjoy. My name's Harry, do you live around here?"

Ruth extended her hand. "Yes, I do. I've lived on the mesa for all my life, almost. There was a time when I went away, but then... well, uh, I came back, didn't I?" She laughed and sipped her coffee. "The house is just over on, ah... Greenfield. Yes, Greenfield."

"Good then, Ruth. Why don't you just sit here and enjoy your coffee. The guys will keep you company. I'll fix toast. Be right back." He waved the bass player over. "Something not right here, I think the old dear doesn't know where she is. I'm going to call this in. See if she wants the restroom. Keep smiling."

The bass player nodded and sat down across from Ruth at the table.

"Oh, yes, my Amos was a musician," she said. "He played the oboe and kept up with his lessons for years. One time he played for me at the beach, I remember it was lovely. The seagulls collected in flocks. Amos said the vibrations of the oboe sounded like the chicks calling." She saluted with her cup, traced a waltz beat in the air.

*****

At the agency, Denise took information from the police department. "Ruth has been found. She's at St. Luke's now," she said to her assistant. "Call the house and let them know. I'll call the family attorney."

Charles took the call. He peered over his glasses at Carl, now nearly horizontal on the sofa. "Thank you, officer. Yes. Yes, goodbye. Carl, that was the police department. Your sister has been located, and she's being checked out at St. Luke's Hospital. You, sir, are hung over and hostile, and I want you to wait here, I'll pick Ruth up. You can meet us at the house in about an hour."

"Hell no. I'm not going to the house. Ruth has bats in her belfry, she's been living in la-la land for years."

"Now, Carl. There's no need for you to be so harsh."

"The woman has no backbone. A little tussle in the car after a dance, and she runs off to a convent and hides for years. You tell me, eh? Then she goes back home to live with the folks. Listens to all their drippy love crap day in and day out."

"Your parents were devoted to one another. And Ruth, unselfishly, looked after them for years."

"Yeah, well I got out and I ain't going back. Maybe she should have looked after herself."

"You may be right there. I spoke with Dr. Finney. He hasn't seen her for many months."

"Whatever. I'm going back to the hotel, shower up, and get back to Capistrano. Keep the agency on until this all gets straightened out, or sue their ass if you can. Get another agency if you need to, or park her in the loony bin. I don't care. I've got to get back to my office. And take my name off the damned call list."

\*\*\*\*\*

Charles met the gerontologist-on-call at the hospital. "Mr. Ralphson, the family's attorney, correct? I've spoken with the family doctor. He believes Miss Steven's Alzheimer's may have worsened. She hasn't had a check up for quite some time. She's unharmed, in spite of all the adventure she must have had. Dehydrated and hungry, but overall she's fine."

"That's a relief," Charles said. "The brother had to return home. My office has conservatorship and is authorized to make medical decisions in his absence."

"Good then. She's a lucky girl, no serious injuries. I'll release her to you now, and fax a report to the family doctor. He wants you to bring Miss Stevens in first thing tomorrow."

When Charles entered Ruth's hospital room, she was sitting up in bed eating oatmeal, the valentine sweater around her shoulders.

"Ralph, my dear. It's so good to see you. The firefighters brought me to this hotel, and everyone has been ever so helpful, but I'm ready to go home now."

"Miss Stevens, we were all worried; you've been gone from the house for over twenty-four hours."

"Well, I did take a kind of a long walk, but twenty-four hours, I don't know about that..."

"You were gone overnight, dear."

"Oh, well. A little camping out under the stars, that's all. Please, don't fuss over me. I'm fine, the doctor said so."

"The doctor who just met with you wants you to check in with Dr. Finney tomorrow. I'll have Jeanette from the office take you to the appointment."

"How silly. I'm perfectly well. Sometimes I forget things, that's all."

"You can discuss this with Dr. Finney. He told me you haven't been in to see him for quite a while, Miss Stevens."

"Perhaps. Nevertheless, everything's all right."

"That's grand, Miss Stevens. Why don't I just step into

the hall, you can dress and tell me more about your walk on the way home."

"Oh, thank you, Charles. See you in a moment, then."

Charles returned to the room just as Ruth was putting on the valentine sweater. He helped her into it and smoothed the shoulders.

"You know, my dear, for all you said about me being out overnight, I really had a nice time. I met a sweet girl whose boyfriend had the flu, poor thing. I met children dressed for Halloween, and was even given a small birthday party. I stopped in at the offices of the Hunt Club. I'm sure Grandfather wouldn't care for their new format. I'm sorry you couldn't have been there."

"Don't be concerned dear," Charles said as he escorted Ruth through the lobby and out to his car.

As they drove through the quiet shaded streets toward the mesa, she turned to him and said, "You know, this reminds me of the time Floyd and I got turned around leaving the Memphis Airport. We were lost for hours."

"Memphis has many beautiful old neighborhoods too, doesn't it?"

"Yes, indeed. Say, why don't we stop at the Humane Society? I'll let you buy the dog you've been pestering me about. She'll be a tall gray girl. Her name is Angel."

## Author's Bio: Maggie Pucillo

Maggie Pucillo lives on the central coast of CA with her husband Richard and a rascally cat, Jack. She is a retired elementary school teacher and enjoys volunteer work at a local school.

Her hobbies include, reading, traveling to Baja, and gardening.

Maggie is the co-author of the paranormal romance, A Spiral of Echoes.

## Reflections

by:  Bonnie Kelly

The sun burned bright in the hot summer. A perfect day for a hike in the cool shade of the woods. The trees weren't too far from home and Casey and Jessica could go there to play as often as they liked. They always took only their most important stuff with them. Casey and Jessica put on their backpacks. They knew their lunch was inside. Mom always packed a lunch for each of them. She never told them what she made. That was part of the fun. They would wait until they sat down to eat before they found out what they would have.

Mom stood in the doorway and watched as they started across the yard.

"Come on, Boston," Jessica hollered for her black Lab.

"Let's go, Wyatt," Casey said to his German Shepherd.

The two dogs ran around the side of the house and across the meadow. They loved to go on hikes.

Casey and Jessica turned and waved good-bye to their mom.

"Have fun." She waved back. "And don't forget Dad is taking all of us out for Valentine's Day dinner, so be home on time."

"For sure," said Casey.

When Casey and Jessica reached the big green meadow, the two dogs ran up and gave Casey and Jessica's hands a big lick and then they were off again. They ranged back and forth in the long grass until a jackrabbit jumped up in front of Boston and ran towards the woods. Boston barked. Wyatt barked. Then both dogs took off in a flash, hot on the trail of the rabbit.

"Those dogs are silly," Jessica said and then laughed. "They always chase rabbits, but they never catch them."

"No, but they sure have fun," Casey said.

Casey and Jessica soon reached the trees and followed

the path the dogs had taken.

After the bright sunlight in the meadow, it took their eyes a few minutes to adjust to the darkness of the forest. They couldn't see the dogs, but they heard their barks, so they knew Boston and Wyatt were close by. After their eyes became used to the dim light, they headed into the woods.

"Let's hike up to the big rock by the creek and eat our lunch," Casey said.

As they walked on through the woods, Boston and Wyatt came bounding back. They were panting from their long run. Boston gave Jessica's hand another lick and the two dogs walked along with the children.

Casey loved the dark shadows of the forest. They could hear the birds singing in the trees. A big brown squirrel on a limb overhead chattered at them, and a bad tempered blue jay squawked in anger. They heard a woodpecker's hammering a little distance off.

When they got to the creek, Boston and Wyatt jumped in the water and splashed around.

"Let's go swimming too and cool off," Jessica said.

"You know we have to wait 'til Dad gets home," Casey said. "We're not supposed to swim alone."

Since they were together Jessica figured they weren't alone, but she didn't want to argue today. "Okay."

They sat near a huge boulder and watched the dogs play. All a sudden, the big jackrabbit ran in front of them and Boston left the water in a hurry. Close behind him, Wyatt barked. The dogs chased after the rabbit and all three of them ran around the big rock and disappeared.

"What happened?" Jessica said, "Where did they go?"

Casey had no answer for his sister. "Wyatt. Boston." He called as loud as he could and waited, but the dogs didn't return. "Wyatt. Here boy." His voice rang out in the forest, but his dog didn't come back. "We'd better go look for them."

Jessica followed him. She didn't want to go, but she didn't want to be alone either.

On the other side the big rock Casey could see a muddy

trail left by the dogs. It went into the creek and out the other side to be lost behind bushes. A dead tree lay over the creek.

"Let's walk across that," Casey said and pointed. "We can keep dry."

Jessica stayed right behind him hanging onto his belt. Suddenly she slipped and fell into the water, pulling Casey with her.

They tumbled over and over each other. Down and down into the deep, deep water. They fought, tried to get to the surface, but something pulled them deeper and deeper. They thought they would go down forever, then all of a sudden they stopped and floated ever so gently, until they hit the bottom.

Plop.

They sat up and looked at each other. The funny thing was, they could breathe under the water. Not only could they breathe, they could see clearly. That was strange. When they went swimming and put their heads under the water everything always looked blurry. And what was even stranger, they weren't even wet. Their clothes were dry. Their hair was dry. Even their backpacks were dry.

"Casey, what happened?"

"I don't know." Casey looked around. He could see they were still in the forest, but everything was upside down. The trees all stood on their tops. The ground looked blue and the sky was brown. A bird flew by close to the blue ground and it flew upside down. The jackrabbit jumped out of some upside down bushes and hopped over their heads, and it was upside down. Suddenly Boston and Wyatt jumped out of the same bushes and chased the rabbit, but the dogs weren't upside down.

"Wyatt. Boston," Casey called, but the dogs kept right on running as if they didn't hear.

Casey got on his feet, grabbed his sister by the hand and they ran after the dogs. Casey and Jessica ran until they were out of breath and too tired to take another step. They had no choice. They had to stop and rest.

When they finally caught their breath, Jessica said,

"Casey, where are we?"

Casey didn't have an answer for his sister. He had no idea where they were.

"I'm scared. I want to go home."

"So do I," Casey said, but he wasn't sure how to get there. He hid his fear from his little sister. Besides, he didn't want to go home without his dogs. "Let's find Boston and Wyatt. Then we'll go home."

They ran some more, following the path they figured the dogs must have taken. The path took a sharp turn and when Casey and Jessica turned with it, they ran right into a little boy. All three went sprawling.

Casey and Jessica got to their feet.

The other boy did too, but he stood on his head. Well, not exactly stood on his head. It was more like he was just upside down, his head where his feet should be, his feet where his head should be. In fact, they were talking to his feet.

"yhW era uoy gnidnats no ruoy daeh?" the boy said.

Jessica looked at Casey. "What did he say?"

"I don't know," Casey turned to the boy. "Why are you standing on your head?"

The boy just looked at them. It was clear he couldn't understand them either.

"Oh, what is the matter?" Jessica cried. "Everything is upside down, we don't know where we are, and now we don't even know what he is saying."

What is the matter? Casey thought. If everything is upside down, and we aren't, then maybe something is the matter with us. Maybe if I was upside down things would look different. If he can walk around like that, maybe I can too. Here goes. He leaned forward, and kicked his legs out behind him. Up they went, until he stood just like the boy.

Casey glanced around. Things did look more normal now.

"Who are you and why do you talk so funny?" the boy said, and this time Casey understood him.

Jessica was still standing up and when the boy spoke, she heard him say, "ohW era ouy dna yhw od ouy klat os ynnuf?

"Why doesn't he speak English?" Jessica said, "and how did you do that? You're upside down now too, Casey."

Casey said, "fI ouy dnats noruoy daeh ouy nac dnatsrednu nih."

"Now you're talking funny," Jessica screamed.

Casey looked at Jessica like he didn't understand a word she said. Then he smiled and turned himself over. Now he stood next to Jessica, right-side up, but everything else was upside down again.

"If you turn yourself over, you will understand him too. Try it."

"Casey, I'm not any good at standing on my head. You know that."

"It's different here. Just bend forward, and kick your legs up behind you. Like this." And Casey showed Jessica how.

She took a deep breath and did as Casey showed her. Then Jessica was also upside down.

"See, now everything looks normal," Casey said.

"Well, now you're making sense," the boy said. "For a while there I thought something was wrong with you. You must know the rules around here. People are not allowed to be upside down. The law is very strict about that."

Jessica didn't want to break any laws, and she was upside down, so she quickly turned herself over.

The boy shouted at her. "s'ehS gniod ti niaga. s'tI ton dewolla. s'tI ton dewolla."

Casey was still on his head so he heard the boy say, "She's doing it again. It's not allowed. It's not allowed."

Casey took his sister's hand and motioned for her to turn over again.

Jessica wasn't sure about doing so. She didn't want to break any laws, but she couldn't understand what they were saying, so she turned over again. "He said it was against the law to be upside down, but he is, and he's telling us to do the same. He doesn't make any sense at all."

"I think he does," Casey said. "If he's upside down, and everything else is upside down, then it all seems right-side up to him, and when you are in a strange place, you should always try your best to do like those around you do, so stay upside down while I talk to him. I wonder if you could help us," Casey said to the boy. "We lost our dogs, one's a black Lab and one is a German Shepherd."

"Dogs? You have dogs? Dogs are not allowed. You stand upside down, and you have dogs. What kind of people are you? I should report you, but I don't want any trouble for myself, so I think I'll just leave as quickly as I can and pretend I never saw you." With that the boy took off very fast.

"Wait," Casey cried. "Come back."

"I don't know what's going on," Jessica said. "I'm scared and hungry, and I want to go home."

"Well, we can't go home just yet," Casey said, "but if you're hungry, we still have the lunch Mom fixed for us. Let's turn back over. I don't know if I can eat upside down."

So they did.

"That feels so much better," Jessica said.

"Let's sit here and eat and maybe we can figure out what to do," Casey said.

They dug around in their backpacks for their sandwiches.

"Oh look," Jessica said, "my sandwich looks like a heart."

"So does mine," Casey said. "Mom must have made them that way because today is Valentine's Day."

"Yes, and we're supposed to be home before Dad gets there because he's taking us all out for that special Valentine dinner tonight, remember? So, we have to get out of here as soon as we can."

They felt much better after they ate and almost forgot about their problems, but then they heard barking off in the distance.

"That sounds like Boston," Jessica said.

"Yes, and Wyatt too. Hurry, let's find them. We have to get them out of here. Who knows what will happen to them if dogs aren't allowed."

They took off down the path.

"If we see any more people," Casey said, "don't forget to turn upside down."

After they ran for quite a long way, Casey and Jessica came out of the woods, and there in front of them stood a small village. All of the houses were upside down. They could still hear the dogs barking off in the distance, and so could everyone in the town.

All the people of the village were running around upside down and yelling. "!sgoD I raeh sgod. ohW dluow era dot tel sgod emoc dnuora ereh? llaC eht ecilop."

"What are they yelling about," Jessica asked.

"Quick, turn yourself over," Casey said. "We don't want them to see us upside down."

When they turned over they heard, "Dogs. I hear dogs. Who would dare to let dogs around here? Call the police."

Two of the villagers ran up to Casey and Jessica. "Have you seen any dogs?"

"No," Casey said, and the villagers ran off. "Quick, let's get back in the woods."

Once they were away from the village, Casey turned over. "You can turn over now. No one can see us."

Jessica was scared and had her eyes closed so she didn't see him.

"uoY nac nrut revo won," he said. "oN eno nac ees su."

Jessica opened her eyes. She saw that Casey had turned over and she did the same. "Will you please not do that anymore?" she said. "Tell me what you just said."

I said, "You can turn over now. No one can see us."

Jessica turned over again. "I wish d'uoy ekam pu ruoy dnim."

Casey grabbed her and made her stand in the same direction he was standing. "What did you say?"

"I said, I wish you'd make up your mind already. Turn over. Stand on your head. Don't stand on your head. I'm so mixed up I don't know which end is up anymore. This place is making me mad. I'm even too mad to be scared. Let's go find Boston and Wyatt and then we can go home, and I am not going to stand on my head anymore."

With that, she marched out of the woods and straight toward the village.

"Jessica, turn upside down."

"I won't. This is me."

Casey followed closed behind. He might not always agree with her, but after all, she was his sister and he couldn't let her face this thing alone.

When they walked from the woods, all the people stopped running around and stared at them.

Jessica marched right into the middle of the village and shouted. "All we want are Boston and Wyatt and then we will go home."

But of course, no one could understand her. All the people heard was, "llA ew era notsob dna ttayw dna neht ew nac og emoh."

The villagers began to whisper amongst themselves and then someone shouted, "eciloP. teG eht ecilop."

A loud whistle blew. Soon Casey and Jessica were surrounded by big upside down men in dark blue uniforms. They looked like policemen.

"s'tahW pu?" The men all spoke at once.

Casey and Jessica couldn't understand them, but they sounded like they meant business.

"I think we'd better turn ourselves over," Casey said, "so we know what they want."

He did and with a loud sigh Jessica did so too.

"You must know the rules around here," a strapping big policeman said. "People aren't allowed upside down. The law is very strict about that. We will have to arrest you now."

"But," Casey said.

"Oh, no buts or ands or maybes about that," a skinny policeman said. "Oh no. Oh no. It's not allowed."

"All we want to do is find our dogs so we can go home," Jessica said.

"Dogs. You have dogs? Dogs are not allowed. Arrest them. Arrest them quick, they have dogs."

The policemen took out their handcuffs and slapped

them on Casey and Jessica's wrists.

"Come along. Come along. Tsk. Tsk," the skinny policeman said and shook his head. "Just think of it. Dogs."

"You can't arrest us," Casey said, "It's Valentine's Day where we live, and our parents are taking us out to dinner."

"Well, oh my, it's Valentine's Day here too, so I know how important that can be. Let's get those handcuffs off, and we will help you find your dogs, then you will see what we mean about dogs."

They removed the handcuffs, but as Jessica turned away she tripped over Casey's foot and stumbled forward. The skinny policeman tried to catch her, but he tripped too. Casey and the big policeman tried to help and they fell too.

Everyone tumbled this way and turned that way and no one could understand anything anyone was saying.

"Watch tuo. kooL tuo. They're getting yawa. Ouch, that's my toof."

Finally, they all managed to turn upside down at the same time.

"That's it," the skinny policemen said. "We were going to let you go, being it's Valentine's Day and all, but you knocked me down. You'll both have to be arrested. It's..."

At that very moment Jessica yelled, "You're all very rude."

Everyone stopped what they were doing and stared at her.

"They sure look mad now," Casey said.

"Did you say rude?" the big strapping policeman said.

Jessica stamped her foot."Yes, and I meant it too."

"Oh dear. Oh my. We didn't mean to be rude. It's against the law to be rude. We just want everyone to obey the rules."

"Well," Casey said. "First a person has to know the rules before he can obey them."

"That's true. How true," the skinny policeman said. "Can't obey the rules if you don't know them."

"Why is it against the rules to be upside down," Casey asked.

"It's clear, isn't it?" the big strapping policeman said. "No one can understand you when you're upside down. It's all too confusing."

"That seems reasonable," Casey said.

"But why aren't dogs allowed," Jessica asked.

"That's quite clear too, isn't it?" the big strapping policeman said.

"Not to me," Jessica answered.

"It's because they always stand on their heads."

"That's silly. Dogs can't stand on their heads."

"Of course they do. When we find yours we will show you."

So, all the upside down policemen and all the upside down villagers helped Jessica and Casey search for their dogs. When they finally found Boston and Wyatt they were running through the upside down woods chasing the upside down rabbit.

"You see. We told you," the skinny policeman said. "They are upside down."

And Casey and Jessica had to agree. Because they were still upside down, everything looked right-side up, except for Boston and Wyatt.

"I see your point," Casey said. "Now if you can show us the way to go home, we'll take our dogs and they won't bother you anymore."

All the policemen and the people of the village showed Casey and Jessica the way to go home. They took them back to the woods to an upside down bush next to a big upside down rock.

"Just step through there," the big strapping policeman said, "hold your breath and kick real hard."

"Good-bye and thank you," Casey and Jessica said, and they gave their dogs a push through the bush. Then they stepped behind the bush, held their breath and kicked very hard.

At first it was dark, but they weren't scared because they could look back and see the people waving at them and they heard them say, "Ho yb eht yaw, yppaH s'enitnelaV yaD!

Even backwards and upside down they knew what that

meant, and they called back, "Happy Valentine's Day to you too."

Soon they saw sunlight shining on the water above them. The next thing they knew, they were standing next to their very own creek, and when they looked around, everything was right-side up, just as it should be.

Boston and Wyatt splashed around in the water and chased their own tails until they spotted a right-side up rabbit and took after it.

Casey and Jessica sat in the warm sun and dried out their clothes, for this time, they were all wet, and that too was as it should be.

After they were dry, they hurried home and arrived just as their dad drove in the yard from work.

"Oh Dad, you must come see. There's an upside down world in the creek." Casey and Jessica said at the same time, and they dragged their father along to the woods.

When they got to the creek their dad looked around, but he didn't see anything strange. "That's just your reflection in the water, kids."

"You have to stick your head in," Casey said, and the three of them did.

But Casey and Jessica couldn't see anything, because everything under the water was blurry.

"Everything is like it always is," Dad said. "Now let's head for home."

When Casey and Jessica stopped to look back, they could see the upside down world in the water.

"Dad, look…" Casey said. But just then Boston and Wyatt jumped in the water to play and the reflection disappeared. "That's why the dogs are never upside down," he said. "They are always playing in the water and never get to see their reflections."

"Hurry," Dad said. "It's time to take Mom out for our Valentine's Day dinner, and then later I bet she'll have our favorite for dessert—pineapple-upside-down cake." He turned and started for home.

Jessica looked at Casey and said, "I bet those people

down there have pineapple-right-side-up cake for dessert."

They laughed, called Boston and Wyatt and followed their dad.

### Author's Bio: Bonnie Kelly

Born in Chicago, Bonnie Kelly has also called Michigan, Arizona, Washington and Hawaii home. Over the last forty years, she has lived throughout California and finally settled on the Central Coast in Northern Santa Barbara County. Bonnie has worked in various areas such as folding billboard posters, working as a file clerk and waitress, stocking shelves, hairdressing, bartending, being a housewife and working as a certified structural welder in the Boilermaker's Union. She even worked at the Dole Pineapple Cannery in Honolulu for 20 minutes and had the pay stub to prove it. Bonnie also published and ran a small town newspaper for over five years, and managed to earn an A.S. degree in Library Science. She has also had two western novels published under the name B.A. Kelly.

## Fiesta Fiascos

by: Pat Prate

"Good morning my name is Dougie Donaldson. Welcome, this is Fiesta Fiascoes, the show where we all get a good laugh from people's foibles during a holiday or special event. Joining me today are our guests, the Mack family from Arizona. For those of you new to our show, let me explain how this works. I will introduce each of them, and they'll get to say a brief hello. I'll then start asking questions of each family member regarding the event that went drastically wrong.

"Let's start on the end, with the dad and work our way down. Introduce yourself to our audience, and tell us what you do for a living. "

"Hi my name is Randi Mack, and this used to be a whole family, Dougie. At the time of this fiasco, I drove a truck, making local deliveries. Since then, I have been driving long-haul, over the road."

"Okay, let's go on to this pretty lady seated next to you. What's your name?"

"My name's Clare Mack, and I'm the youngest daughter. At the time, I was in high school. I now work in law enforcement."

"Randi, we seem to be surrounded by pretty ladies today. Who's this in the middle?"

"I'm May, the oldest. This whole thing was my idea, sorry to say. I was in college when I thought this up. I'm in the military reserves, currently living in Rhode Island."

"On the end I suppose we have Mrs. Mack who was the victim in all this?"

"Yes. Victim. I'm Doris Potter. I have since resumed using my maiden name. I'm currently between jobs."

"Doris, you don't appear very happy to be here today."

"Well, Dougie, I'm not. I would rather not relive the experience, but my wishes got overturned by the rest of the family. It's always the same."

"We'll try to make it as painless as possible for you, Doris. All right now that the introductions are over, let's start at the beginning. May, you said this whole thing was your idea, so why don't we let you begin. Tell us why you thought this up in the first place and how it unraveled from your perspective."

"I'm a little nervous Dougie. I've never been on television before so pardon me if I make a few mistakes or cry while I recall the details. Our Mom's birthday is February fifteenth. Depending on what may be happening in a particular year, our family would celebrate both her birthday and Valentine's Day together as one party. I knew she always felt a little shortchanged because of this so I decided for her 40th birthday we should be extravagant.

"At the time I worked in the mall to help pay my school bills, and the store across the walkway was a party store. During one of my breaks, I went over and browsed through the birthday supplies. I came across a package designed for a woman's 40th birthday. Everything was black, the crêpe paper, the stars, even the sign which said happy birthday. Immediately I envisioned the whole house decorated in black with sayings like *'Over The Hill'* and *'You're Not Going To Make It'*. My sister and I have always joked with Mom, and we thought it would be a funny little surprise.

"When I got home that day, I conspired with my sister in our bedroom about the decorations. Dad heard us, and chimed in with his two cents. He said we should get a cake decorated the same way with black frosting. Our conspiracy was beginning to take shape. Clare suggested we should have flowers as well, and make it a surprise party with the neighbors invited. All that remained was to delegate the duties and make sure Mom stayed away from the house long enough to put up the decorations and bring the cake in."

"Thank you May. I'm sorry to interrupt right here, but we have to go to commercial break. When we return, let's hear Clare's version of the events. You're listening to Fiesta Fiascoes, and I'm your host, Dougie Donaldson. We'll be right back

***** 

"Welcome back to Fiesta Fiascoes. We're talking with the Mack family about a birthday and Valentine's Day that went very wrong. Clare, what was your role in all of this?"

"Well, like May said, she came home after work all bubbly about this plan for a surprise party for Mom. I had just planned to get Mom a box of chocolates and a nice card, but a surprise party along with it started my juices flowing. May is the one who can decorate a house in two seconds flat, so I suggested I take the responsibility to keep Mom away from the house for the afternoon."

"Let me interrupt you a minute. Tell our audience how much time in advance, this planning took."

"Oh, sorry Dougie. We started this planning on Monday afternoon. Valentine's Day was Friday and Mom's birthday, Saturday. The only other thing I had to do was to make sure Mom was distracted whenever we needed to get together to discuss the logistics of our plan, or if we wanted to sneak something into the house."

"I see. We haven't heard from Randi yet. Tell us your version of what happened."

"Thank you, Dougie. Well, like May said, I happened to be walking by their bedroom and heard them discussing a surprise for Doris. I have always been one to try to camouflage a present or hide it so the recipient finds it unexpectedly. The minute I heard them talking about it I asked, 'How can I help'? We immediately decided May would order the cake, and I would pick it up on my way home from work, Friday. I would also be responsible for stopping at the florist and picking up the flowers, namely a dozen black roses. It turns out you can't get black roses. They have a very dark colored one, and that's as close as you can get to black. I had to settle.

"My daughters didn't know it at the time, but I had received a windfall payment the week before. I suggested we try to book a weekend getaway for me and Doris, even if it was short notice. A few calls and presto-chango, I managed to book us on the train from Williams, Arizona to the Grand Canyon, with an overnight stay in Grand Canyon Village at one of the motels. It turns out most of the United States at that time was focused on Kansas City due to a worldwide sporting event having their finals there that particular weekend. The Grand Canyon was empty and offered screaming deals. I also booked a rental car for the two hour drive to Williams, Arizona and back."

"Randi, let me interrupt again. Tell the folks where you were living at the time and remind us what you were doing at your job."

"Oh, right, Dougie. We were living in Verde Valley, Arizona and I was working as a local delivery driver, which is where the complications came in."

"Hold that thought, Randi. We have to take another commercial break. We haven't heard from Doris yet so when we return, she'll tell us how she felt about this whole birthday bash."

*****

"Welcome back. We're visiting with the Mack family, and Doris is about to tell us what happened on her 40th birthday that went so wrong."

"Well Dougie, I've actually never been one who enjoys extended surprises. I don't mind a little popper on my plate with a gift inside or maybe a piece of candy, but withholding my birthday from me goes beyond my ability to enjoy it."

"Doris, explain yourself. Do you feel people who create elaborate surprises like your family did, don't understand you? Do you feel put upon, or they are taking advantage of you?"

"No, Dougie. It's not that. Ever since I was a little girl, whoever arranged my birthday party always included Valentine's Day. I get tired of always using somebody else's holiday for my birthday. When people don't even notice it's coming along, it really irritates me. This particular time nobody mentioned it at all. The days were getting closer and I didn't get one happy birthday. Not a card, not a kiss, not a hug, nothing but day to day humdrum. Girls to school, Randi to work, then everybody home again for supper every day. I was beginning to think the whole world had forgotten about me."

"I see. Did any of the rest of you notice Doris was becoming irritated the closer it came to the big day? Clare. You raised your hand. What are your thoughts?"

"Without spilling the beans, every night at supper I would mention that Mom and I should go shopping for some new clothes on Friday afternoon. I had a half day of school and I tried to make it look like a mother-daughter bonding experience, but I didn't mention Valentine's Day or her birthday. I could tell something was wrong Friday morning. I thought maybe she had caught a bug or something. She just seemed a little out of sorts."

"Doris, let's go back to you. Did you want to go shopping with Clare on Valentine's Day afternoon?"

"I have to tell you, Dougie, by the time we left the house to go shopping; I would just as soon have crawled under the covers of our bed and stay there all weekend. I was really beginning to feel left out and forgotten."

"Okay. May, did you also have a half day of school?"

"Yes I did. This is part of the reason why I came up with a plan in the first place. I knew there would be time enough to decorate the house and get the flowers and cake in place. We also wanted to make sure Mom didn't see any of the neighbors come into the house for the party."

"Back to Randi. You had to work on Friday correct? What time did you get home?"

"Yeah, Dougie. I had to work and this is where all our plans started to fall apart. On any given Friday, I would get off between three and four PM. This particular day, maybe because it was Valentine's Day and there were extra deliveries, I didn't get off until almost five o'clock. I had to rush to the florist because they closed at five thirty and I also had to hurry to the bakery and pick up the cake.

"In the meantime, May kept calling me about every fifteen minutes. asking me my location and when will I be home? Since May stayed at the house to decorate, she also acted as dispatch central. As long as I wasn't home, she kept telling Clare to extend the shopping trip. By the time I got home Friday night, it was almost six thirty. Traffic was not my friend that day. I had to drop the cake and flowers at the house, then go pick up the rental car. May drove me over to the agency, but when we got there, the car I had reserved was gone. Why they do things like that, I'll never understand. The only other car available was a luxury model which required an additional $350 cash deposit. Since the banks were closed and I hadn't deposited my check yet, I had to use the funds set aside for the trip. All this took extra time, so it was almost seven thirty before we got back to the house.

"May called Clare before we left the rental agency so we could time everybody getting to the house together."

"Let me interrupt your thoughts here for a minute Randi."

"Sure, Dougie. What is it?"

"You mentioned all these problems getting the rental car. Why didn't you just use your personal vehicle?"

"Good question Dougie. I skipped over that part. As I mentioned before I received a windfall. It was an insurance settlement because our car got totaled in an accident. The only other vehicle we had to use was my work truck. It's as big as a *U-Haul* van, and painted the color of a school bus. It also get's lousy mileage. It didn't have a heater, or air conditioning. Not exactly the vehicle you want for a romantic weekend."

"I see, Randi. I don't think my wife would want me taking her out to dinner in a truck like that either. Okay we're going to take another break here. When we come back, we'll talk to Doris again about some of the surprises you had in store for her."

*****

"Welcome back. Our guests are the Mack family. Doris is going to tell us about these particular surprises. Doris, why don't you start when Clare invited you to go on a shopping trip for the afternoon."

"All right. At first I thought it would be a fun, mother-daughter day at the mall. I also thought, somewhere along the line, she may buy me a birthday lunch, or card, or something. I also expected to get back to the house by four o'clock. I had plans for the weekend and needed to make the preparations. As the day dragged on and on, I got more and more antsy to get home. In all this time at the mall, Clare never once wished me a happy birthday, or offered to buy me even a birthday roll, or a cup of coffee, let alone lunch. By the time we got home, I was more than a little bit peeved and very hungry. I felt like my whole birthday afternoon had been stolen from me."

"You were having an *un*happy birthday. Is that correct?"

"Yes, Dougie. I thought everyone had forgotten about me and my day. All I wanted to do was crawl in a hole and pull a rock over me."

"Let me talk to May for a minute. When your sister came home from the mall with Doris, you and Randi were just returning from the rental car agency. Is that correct?"

"Yes, Dougie. I had spent the whole afternoon decorating the house. The cake was on the kitchen table with two huge candles on it, which looked like gravestones. One had a four, the other a zero. The flowers were in vase next to the cake. We had a folding card table set up in the kitchen as well, with presents and cards on it from family, friends, and neighbors. The idea was, when Mom got home, and came into the kitchen, everyone would yell, surprise."

"May, quick question. If Doris and Clare were at the mall, and you two were picking up the rental car, how were the friends and neighbors going to hide in your house?"

"I'm sorry. I left that detail out didn't I? We lived in a very friendly neighborhood. Most of the neighbors had keys to everybody else's houses. When we realized how late we were, getting the party started, I called Hannah Kassel, who lived directly across from us. She house sits for us when we're gone. When guests arrived, she invited them in and explained our minor snafu."

"Okay, so the decorations are all set and everyone is arriving about the same time. Clare, you continue with the story when Doris entered the kitchen and noticed the decorations."

"Dougie, it wasn't the happy scene May and I had planned. Mom looked at everything and started crying, even before we could all yell surprise. She mumbled something about not being that old. We hit a nerve by accident and it was too late to do anything about it. I looked at May, then at Daddy, and the three of us shrugged our shoulders in unison. We decided to make the best of it, passing out cake and having Mom open her presents one at a time. We decided to save Dad's present for last, because it was supposed to be the biggest and best."

"Interruption again, Clare. What exactly happened when Doris opened the present with the weekend trip in it?"

"I'll tell you, if ever a birthday could go wrong, this was it. Mom opened the card and really began to cry. At first, we all thought they were tears of joy, but we were wrong. She started hollering at Daddy about all her plans for the weekend. May and I chimed in together that a surprise is just that. Plans need to change, occasionally."

"Doris, what did you think would happen if you canceled your original plans for the weekend?"

"First, like I said before, I felt like my birthday had been hijacked. Second, I belong to a group of women who meet occasionally, away from the menfolk, to have a good time just talking about women things. This particular weekend, it was my turn to host the group. I felt I would be letting them down by not living up to my responsibilities. It's not that I didn't want to go away for a weekend with my husband. I needed more time to plan for it."

"Doris, every time you talk about doing something, it involves a planning stage. Could it be you are reluctant to let other people plan events for you?"

"Maybe. I don't know. I was really beginning to feel like my whole weekend was gone."

"Back to Randi for a minute. Why don't you describe the trip next? We know the whole party went down in flames, but maybe the actual trip you had planned could resurrect your weekend."

"Not so fast, Dougie. The actual ride up to Williams,

Arizona was rather chilly, and I don't mean temperature. Almost the whole way, Doris looked out the passenger window and didn't say more than two words to me. When we actually got to the train, all the other people milling around, looking forward to a happy ride up to the Grand Canyon, turned her mood around a little.

"We settled into our seats and we finally started talking and laughing. I'll tell you though, the saying about if it wasn't for bad luck I wouldn't have any, was really holding true that weekend. About halfway between Williams and the Grand Canyon, the engine on the train broke down. We sat there for almost 2 hours while another engine was prepared and brought up to us. Because of the way the tracks are made up there, the spare engine had to come up from Williams on the sidetrack, go almost up to the Grand Canyon, then come back down on our track to hook onto the front of the train. When we finally got to the Grand Canyon, we no longer had enough time to see any of the sites. We took our luggage to the motel, only to find out that because we had been delayed, our reservation had been canceled. The manager told us he would do what he could to find us a room for the night, but it may be another couple of hours. Because I had to use my cash for the rental car, I had to cancel the reservation we had for dinner in the fancy restaurant. The snack bar which sells hot dogs, hamburgers, and other hot sandwiches had already closed for the day. Our big dinner consisted of going to a machine to get one cold sandwich, chips and drinks. The rest of the time at Grand Canyon didn't get much better. On the train trip back to Williams, the engine broke down again. For most of the ride home, I got a wonderful view of Doris' hair, as she pressed her face toward the passenger window."

"Wow, Randi. Talk about from bad to worse. Do these things follow you around on a regular basis?"

"Sometimes it feels like it, Dougie, but not usually."

"Time for another commercial break. When we return, I want to get Doris' reaction to the snafus that happened up at Grand Canyon and Williams."

*****

"Welcome back. Doris, give us your version of the train ride, the motel, the dinner, everything."

"Thanks, Dougie. I was wondering when I would get my chance to tell it. Randi's right. I did kind of ignore him on the ride to Williams. All things considered, I was still a little miffed about what had happened the day before. When we got to Williams, and started mingling with the rest of the people who would be on the train, I actually started to enjoy myself. It's when the train broke down that things turn sour. I am not one who believes in *plan B.* I get frustrated when the original plans don't work out the way they should. When we finally got to the Grand Canyon, and things started going sour up there as well, my mood took a nosedive. We finally did get a motel room, but it was several hours later. I locked myself in the bathroom and cried for more than an hour. I just felt hurt. When I finally came out, I didn't get into the same bed as Randi. I pulled the covers over my head and cried myself to sleep while he watched a movie on television. The next morning was no better. Like Randi said, the train broke down again, and I felt like climbing under the wheels and letting it roll over me. It's no wonder I didn't want to talk to anyone during the car ride home."

"What happened when you got back home? Did things return to normal?"

"No Dougie, they didn't. Randi went back to work, the kids went back to school, and I still felt like I had been abandoned and misused. Nobody noticed."

"I see. We're almost out of time, so I want to let Randi be the one who wraps this up. Any last thoughts on this Fiesta Fiasco weekend of yours?"

"One last thought Dougie. Doris never did get out of the funk this weekend caused her. About five months later, on our anniversary, I came home to find divorce papers laying on the seat of my chair with a note saying she was going to live with her father, in California. In the space of about six months, I went from happily married to divorced, with no clue."

"Talk about surprises, Randi. That last bit took me completely off guard. Our show is supposed to be informal and upbeat. That's one heck of a downer note to leave this on, but as I said before, we're out of time. Until we meet again, this is Dougie Donaldson saying we hope your fiestas don't become fiascoes like this one. Goodbye, everybody."

### Author's Bio:  Pat Prate

Pat Prate worked as a long haul truck driver for more than fifteen years. While on the road, his first book, was published in 2010.

Due to the economy and the price of fuel, his company went out of business in April of 2011.

He intended to drive semi-trucks forever, but instead retired and turned to writing novels. He lives on the Central Coast of California, caring for his mother. He also enjoys football, NASCAR and their cat, a Siamese mix. His current novel, Semi-Sleuth, about life on the road, will published soon.

Other books by Pat Prate: The D-E System; Joe Driver's Trip; The Autobiography of an Invisible Man (humor).

E-mail address: spr8502@hotmail.com

## Looking For Love in the Wrong Place?

by

Helen Jacobsen

Most singles are all too aware of the wrong places to look for love. (Bars, Aunt Mable's next door neighbor's 52 year old son still living in the basement, Obits for newly single) That perfect someone won't come knocking at the door while you are sitting at home complaining about how hard it is to meet other singles.

Here are some ideas for you to try to find love. Perhaps even by Valentine's Day.

Get out of the house. Interact with singles groups, place an ad in your local paper, or on-line. Come up with funny quips to catch their attention and to ensure responses.

Go where the singles are:

a) You find ladies at aerobic and yoga classes, shopping malls, or evening college classes.

b) You find men at sporting events, Laundromats, or fly fishing classes.

When going out don't always hang out with your buddies or girlfriends. Lots of people are very shy. It is easier to approach one smiling face than to single out one attractive person in a group.

So go alone to the places where the type of single person you might be interested in go, this could be anything from co-ed baseball to a singles church social.

Don't be overly concerned about your appearance. Some women may be more concerned about their nails than relationships. Perhaps the nails have lasted longer. Overly made up women look like they are high maintenance. Believe it or not even more important than looks, is someone comfortable to be with. Go where the possibilities are!

Initiate contact. It doesn't do any good to go out to the right place if you don't make contact when you're there.

We all fear rejection, so much so that we often don't ever take the first step to meet someone. Without that step you will only meet the small percentage that has the courage to come to you. It is a two way street.

Statistically, you have to meet lots of people to find the right one, and if singles are frozen in the initiation step there is dramatically less chance of that ever happening. There are really lots of wonderful available single people out there. The numbers don't lie. Forty-two percent of U.S. people are single (80 million) it is the fastest growing segment of our population.

PS. If you do meet a special someone it will take a year to really get to know each other, the good and bad, at least six more months to know each other's families. Then there is the wedding to plan, another six months, so don't book the church just yet.

Enjoy the journey, take your time, it could save you both the pain of a false start. It is very easy to fall in love but harder to have the patience to let your love prove itself before hopping into bed, moving in together, or rushing into marriage.
.

With sense of humor, practical advice and valuable motivation, you too can have a shot at finding love by Valentine's Day.

### Author's Bio:  Helen Jacobsen

Helen Jacobsen is an adventure in herself. She has had articles published in the *Fresno Friends* single magazine and has  worked as a stringer for seven different news papers for over twenty years.

She has taught photography, travel, and finance, classes at Cal Poly in the Ollie program and now for the lifelong Learners of the Central Coast (LLCC), and has traveled the world with her *Financially Smart* seminars.

All of this fun variety gives her a substantial base for writing short stories, articles, and her new book, *Handbook For Singles.*

She lives in Arroyo Grande and enjoys the fabulous variety of outdoor activities our beautiful central coast offers.

## The Birth of The Santa Maria California Word Wizards

In 1994 author Elaine Bierbaurer moved to Santa Maria, CA. Among the things she left behind was an active writers group. Needing one for her creative outlet, she set out to form one in her new hometown.

She and a fellow resident of Casa Grande Mobile Estates, Sylva Mularcyk, sought out fellow authors, and what would become *The Santa Maria California Word Wizards* came into being.

The first meeting of *Word Wizards* happened at *Café Monet* with five core members. Three of the five are still part of the group.

At first, *Word Wizards* met on Tuesday evenings. And they still do, but a year ago a daytime group started. Eighteen years later, the meetings are still held at the same café, which now is called *Café Noir*.

*Word Wizards* has grown to sixteen core members, all talented authors.

Around the same time as the day group formed, one of the authors, Barbara M. Hodges, who attends both the day and the night meetings, suggested an idea.

"Why not do a Word Wizards anthology? We'll choose a theme, and write stories and poetry containing the theme. I suggest Valentine's Day."

Valentine's Day as a theme wasn't greeted with enthusiasm.

Responses came: "I don't write romance."

"It's too much of a hearts-and-flowers day."

That's when Barbara presented the challenge. "We can do it differently. There's much more to love then hearts and flowers. Write something different. The only have-to-be is a mention of Valentine's Day."

There was still much skepticism until Aubry Johnson

brought in his story, *Baby Bottles*. In his story of a young Viet Nam pilot, the others saw how Valentine's Day could be the theme of stories beyond the traditional.

Fourteen authors said, "I can do that." And they did. Now it was time to find a title that did justice to the stories and Sylva Mularcyk suggested *Scattered Hearts*. The group approved. It said it all; the stories involve the heart and are scattered across many states and times. We know you will enjoy a different look at the day dedicated to love.